the roommates

Three Player Grind Book 1

allyson lindt

acelette press

For my eternal dragon

1
daria

I'D SAT in board meetings for some of the wealthiest companies in the world, looked their CEOs in the eye, and told them they were being fucking idiots and would be the reason they're company went under.

And I never broke a sweat.

But I was in a near panic over sending my daughters to Disneyland.

Sure, I sent them to their dad's every weekend, and all four of us had gone to Disneyland together when I was still married to Joe and the girls were younger. But this time he was taking them to the park by himself.

I stood in the middle of the living room, their luggage in front of me, and resisted the urge to check their suitcases a third time, to make sure we hadn't forgotten to pack anything.

Harmony was dancing around me, singing something that had started off as *Bippity, Boppity, Boo,* segued to *A Whole New World*, and was now *Be Our Guest*. She stopped immediately in front of me, eyes wide, and expression somber. "Mom. What if Cinderella isn't there when we go to her castle?"

"Then you'll have to check back later."

"But I'll be busy later." Harmony had an entire schedule of where she wanted to go and when, in all the parks. What five-year-old did that?

Mine, apparently. And she'd probably learned it from watching me. "If you ask Alana, she'll make sure you can move your schedule around, okay?"

Harmony scrunched her face up, then grinned. "Okay." Before she could start singing again, a car pulled into the driveway. "*Dad's here*," she shouted, and ran to the front window.

He was five minutes early. I was impressed. It wasn't that Joe was specifically irresponsible. The opposite in fact—if work called, all else was second priority.

I liked to think I wasn't that bad, but there were days I was just as guilty. I was trying, though. My girls deserved one parent who was there for them.

"*Mom*." Alana's cry came from upstairs in reply. "I can't find my navy capris."

"You already packed them."

"Not *those*. The other ones." Alana appeared at the top of the stairs.

Right. I did a quick mental inventory of the house. "Are they in the dryer?"

"Maybe." She ran into the basement, footsteps

heavier than should be possible for a thin thirteen-year-old.

Harmony opened the door as Joe reached the front step, and hugged his legs. "Hi, Daddy."

He ruffled her hair. "Hey, short stuff. You ready to meet Cinderella?"

"*Yeah.*" Harmony clapped.

He looked at me. "I'm sorry about this." He wasn't really.

I'd rearranged my schedule and the girls' specifically to make sure I could take them to Hawaii this week. I didn't believe for a moment that it was a coincidence Joe scheduled a Disneyland trip at the same time, especially when he let me know by asking them to pick which one they preferred.

I gave him my sweetest smile anyway. "I understand. The girls are looking forward to it, and I'm glad they have the chance to go."

"Found them," Alana said from behind me.

I handed Harmony her backpack. "Take this and help Dad load your stuff into the car." I nudged the heaviest suitcase toward Joe.

Joe grabbed the bag, and followed Harmony outside.

When they were out of earshot, I turned to Alana. "Promise me you'll keep an eye on Harmony."

"Mom. You already know." Alana huffed.

"Say it anyway. Reassure me you'll make sure she gets to go on the rides she wants."

Alana crossed her arms. "What about the rides I want to go on?"

"Make sure Dad lets you go on those too."

She raised her brows. "So if he's ignoring us, do I have permission to call him a dickhead?"

It was so tempting. "Don't call your father a dickhead to his face." That was a reasonable concession. "And you're welcome to take his phone and pocket it before you get on rides, to make sure he's focused on Harmony." How fucked up was it that I trusted my twelve-year-old more than my ex-husband?

Then again, there was a reason he was the ex.

We finished loading up Joe's car, strapped Harmony into her booster seat, and I gave the girls one more round of hugs before forcing myself to send them on their way.

That was one pair on their way. Now I just had to get the next one settled, and then I was jetting off to Hawaii on my own. I already had the vacation set up, no reason to stay at home and mope. While I was gone, Alana's swim coaches would be staying here. Their apartment was being fumigated, they were saving every penny they could, to grow their coaching business, and the arrangement made sense.

An exercise in efficiency. It was a beautiful thing. Though I'd still rather be taking the vacation with my daughters.

I loaded up my own things into my car, and was just finishing when Colin parked in front of the house.

Tanner wasn't far behind, taking the second spot in the driveway.

As they climbed out of their vehicles, I knew better than to ogle their well-toned forms. Mostly because I'd had a year or two of practice, and I'd do my staring when they weren't looking. I always felt weird, in a Mrs. Robinson kind of way, objectifying them.

Not that they were kids, but at thirty, they were still nearly a decade younger than me.

"Morning, Ms. Lane," Colin called at the same time Tanner said, "Hey, Daria."

I waved back, never sure which name was more awkward, and nodded at the front door. "Hey guys. Come on in."

As they walked past me, I most definitely drank in an eyeful. They were both dressed in T-shirts and shorts—reasonable, expected, but always a tempting reminder of what they looked like wearing less.

Colin was about six inches taller than my five-six, with broad shoulders, dark hair, and the most adoring brown eyes. I knew from the many times I'd seen him teaching the kids that he had the perfect amount of fuzz on his chest, and deity levels of patience with the students.

Tanner had been an Olympic swimmer, but a torn rotator cuff stopped him from finishing the year he competed, and the injury never healed to the point where he could rejoin the team. He still kept his body mostly hair free, which... *yum*. And he had a piercing blue gaze that made most people crack under it.

There were days when I could convince myself the age difference didn't matter long enough to indulge fantasies about them, but I never managed to forget they were Alana's favorite teachers. A reality that made it easier to keep them as friends and nothing more.

"All right, grand tour." I stopped next to them in the living room. "Our bedrooms are upstairs. Stay out of the girls' rooms unless there's some sort of disaster." I wasn't actually worried about them violating our private spaces, but the checklist was in my head and I was going through it. "You're welcome to use the shower in my room if you need to. You won't run out of hot water, using two at the same time."

I led them into the kitchen. "Help yourself to anything in the fridge and cupboards. Please do, so it doesn't go bad." Two steps down and we were in the sunken family room. I gestured to the two rooms that sat off that. "You can sleep in those. There's another shared shower. Laundry room, weights, and treadmill are downstairs. Help yourself. My office is down there too, and stays locked for client privacy reasons, and not at all because *you should never go in there*." I hoped my light sarcasm conveyed the spooky old movie vibe I was going for.

Their laughs said I'd nailed it.

Was the house entirely too big for three people? Yes. But back when my universe revolved around Joe, we had grand visions of this becoming our lifetime home, retiring here, having plenty of room for grandkids…

I'd been so delusional.

"That's that. You can call me if you need me. Any questions?"

"I think we're set. Thank you so much, again, for letting us stay here," Colin said.

"Of course, no problem." Temptation surged through me, to stick around, chat a little longer. Maybe joke.

I had a flight to catch and if I was lucky, I'd hook up with some hottie on the beach while I was gone. Unlikely he'd be the same kind of company Colin and Tanner were, but I was looking for pretty and a good lay, not late-night conversations under the stars.

"Right. Yeah. Call me." I shouldered my laptop and grabbed my purse.

My phone rang. I glanced at the screen. *Work. Fuck.* "Be right back. So I can leave again," I said to the guys.

I wandered into the front foyer as I clicked *Answer.* "This is Daria."

"Thank God I caught you before your flight." Bernie didn't sound panicked the way his words implied. He'd known I would still be here.

I swallowed my groan. "Only barely. What can I do for you?"

He was one of the partners who owned the angel investment firm I worked for. He was damn good at his job—investing and making a huge return—but he wasn't a people person. "Zedophap is having a series of post go-live vendor issues. I need you to give them a call."

"I'm literally walking out the door to catch a plane." When I took this job right as Joe and I were divorcing, the thought of telling any of the partners *no* would've made me wither and die. I'd had to learn better.

"I need you to take this. If this wasn't a hundred-million-dollar crisis, I wouldn't ask."

Bullshit. "Non-refundable vacation package."

"I'll cover the cost myself. And if you pull this off —which you will—there's a big bonus in it for you."

Damn it. That kind of money would pay for a better vacation. One I could actually enjoy with my daughters. "Fine. Give me ten minutes to set up my laptop and I'll call them."

"Thank you." Bernie's gratitude caught me off-guard.

I held my growl until I disconnected, then let it roll out in a long wave of frustration.

"Everything all right?" Colin's question caught me off guard.

I spun to find him in the doorway, those dark puppy dog eyes watching me with concern.

Right. The other part of this equation was the sexy young studs I'd promised my house to for the next week. How best to phrase this?

2

tanner

I WAS DOING my best not to eavesdrop on Daria's call, despite the growing stress in her voice. But when Colin asked if she was okay, I had to know the answer.

Instead of answering, she was twisting a strand of hair tightly around one finger. It was a rare moment of her looking vulnerable, and that was as sexy as the take-no-shit confidence she normally wore.

A lot of mothers flirted with me, but she was the only one I wished would. I shouldn't be thinking about a student's mom that way, but she was gorgeous, intelligent, had the best dry sense of humor, and I bet she knew exactly what she liked in the bedroom.

"Daria?" I prompted.

She sighed. "My vacation is canceled. I need to use my office for a few hours today, but then I'll grab a hotel and be out of your hair."

Very little of that sentence made sense, but I focused on the least logical part of it. "Why would you get a hotel?"

"Because I promised you two the house for a week."

Was this her version of propriety, or...? I didn't understand. "This is *your* home and it's more than big enough for the three of us.:"

"I don't—"

"He's right." Colin stopped her. "You let us stay here so we wouldn't have to pay for a place to stay. It's a little ridiculous for you to do so instead if you're not leaving town."

Daria twisted her mouth, tempting me with full, luscious lips. "My office *is* here. It's easier for me to keep working from it."

"Issue resolved." In a best-of-all-worlds kind of way, in my opinion. "Go. Work. We promise to be quiet."

One corner of her mouth tugged up. "This means you'll have to cancel whatever wild parties you had planned." A hint of teasing slid into her voice.

Which meant she was already feeling a little better. Good. I gave an exaggerated sigh. "Damn. I guess I'd better start making calls. Telling everyone the fun is over."

She let out a short laugh. "Seriously. This'll sound weird, but thank you."

"It sounds wrong. You don't have to thank us for sharing your house with you." I loosely grasped her shoulders and pointed her toward the basement. "Go. Work. We'll bring your stuff in from the car and leave it in the foyer."

Did I watch her ass as she walked down the stairs? Damn straight. What she did to a pair of business slacks was incredible, but today I had the added bonus of picturing what she would've looked like lounging on the beach in a two-piece. I dragged my gaze away, and Colin and I headed out to bring her luggage back in, then our own stuff.

Of the two rooms available to us, one had a full bathroom, and the other looked like it was meant to be an office, but a bed had been crammed in the corner. I let Colin have the *real* bedroom. I'd be spending enough time at the pool that I would shower there as often as not.

Speaking of, "I'm going to do some laps before class this afternoon," I said. The *if you want to join me* was implied.

"Cool. I'll catch up with you in a few hours."

Colin's answer didn't surprise or concern me. We both loved swimming, but I had a bit more time invested.

I grabbed my gym bag and headed out. It was mid-morning on a Monday, late enough the commute was over but early enough lunch traffic hadn't started, so my drive was casual and quick. It also meant the private pool where we taught was mostly empty.

Perfect. That would make it easier to push myself

11

without interruption. Eight years ago, I'd been lucky enough to make the Olympic swim team. When I tore my rotator cuff during one of my first races, I was furious at myself for being stupid enough to get hurt.

The injury had healed, but I'd been told I'd never compete at that level again. Four years later, I was so far from making the cut, it wasn't funny. According to all the data, I'd been past my peak then. I didn't care —I was going to make the team this year. This was my last chance to live that dream.

I just had to shave three-quarters of a second off my fifty-meter crawl.

I changed into my suit and rinsed off in the shower before stepping into the main pool area. The scent of chlorine was familiar and oddly soothing, and I inhaled the humid warmth. The easiest way to check my time when I was alone was with a water-proof camera on a tripod. I set the device up at one end of the lane, took a few deep breaths, then one to hold, and dove in.

When I burst from the water at the other end, I gasped deeply. A quick check of the recording told me I was still missing my goal. I swam the lane again and again, but no matter how hard I pushed, I couldn't shorten my time. In fact, the longer I tried, the more milliseconds I added to the clock.

My bad shoulder was tight and my lungs burned. I stretched to work through the pain. One more try, and I'd have to call it quits and get ready for our first class.

"*Tanner,*" the pool owner's call shattered my focus.

I shook off the irritation at being interrupted, and turned to face John. "Hey." I kept my smile pleasant. "What's up?"

"I'm not making this public knowledge yet, but since you and Colin have been renting from me for so long, I wanted to give you a heads-up. I'm putting the place on the market, and I can't guarantee the future owners will honor existing contracts."

I barely heard the last part of his sentence because inspiration lit up my thoughts at *putting the place on the market*. Was this the opportunity Colin and I were waiting for? A chance to own our own pool? Grow our business to something more than a couple of guys offering coaching a few hours a week? "Do you have any offers? What's your asking price?"

"Nah. It's just been listed." He gave me a dollar amount.

It was a lot, but far less than we'd pay for our own, and we weren't far from having the down payment for a loan like that. "Thanks for the heads-up." I wanted to add *I'll be in touch with you and your agent*, but not until I talked to Colin.

Now was the perfect time to push hard for funding.

And balance that with me getting ready for the Olympic swim trials, which were less than a month away.

But there was plenty of time for both. I was sure of it.

3

colin

I WAS jealous that Tanner insisted Daria stay.

Which was fucked up on *so many* levels. This was her house. Duh, of course she was going to stay here.

And Tanner was my roommate and business partner, so we saw each other more often than we saw anyone else; this week wasn't special, despite it feeling like a mini-vacation.

Besides, it wasn't as though I was going to tell him how I felt, after all this time. I could picture it now, and it went down the same way it had the billion other times I'd imagined my confession.

Hey, Tanner. I love you. As more than a best friend. I'm talking in an I-want-to-be-the-person-sucking-your-cock-for-the-rest-of-our-lives kind of way.

To which imaginary Tanner always replied, *you know I'm straight, right? I'm sorry, man.*

And then things would get awkward.

I'd lived with that specific *daydream* since we were

teenagers, which meant no matter how much his imagined response was or wasn't founded in reality, it had become part of my own psychological dogma.

My phone rang and my oldest sister's picture showed on the screen.

"Hey," I answered as I headed into my temporary room.

"Hey. You guys screw on the couch yet?" Brooke's tone was bright

I rolled my eyes, grabbing my laptop bag and setting it on the bed. "Nope. And not on the kitchen counter, or against the wall, or… did I miss anything?"

"Sounds like you're missing out on a lot." She meant the teasing in good fun. No one else knew how I felt about Tanner, and I was grateful she both understood and had never said anything to him.

"Tell me about it." I paused. Having her try to helpfully explain the birds and bees to me when I was ten and she was twenty had scarred me enough I remembered the awkwardness almost two decades later. "On second thought, please don't. Eww."

She laughed. "Seriously though, what's your schedule like this week?"

I pulled my computer out, and set it on the barely big enough nightstand. "Well… our hostess had to cancel her vacation, so I have to cancel the orgies." I let out an exaggerated sigh. "But we're staying here anyway. Otherwise, limited class schedule thanks to summer break, and not a clue besides that."

"Do you want a job?"

I tempered my excitement. *A job* meant a chance to paint murals on someone's wall, which I loved. But the details made all the difference. "Who?"

"Antique shop. You have artistic freedom as long as there's no blood or genitalia."

"Are they sure?" My work didn't tend toward graphic, but a lot of people who said *artistic freedom* didn't understand that meant mine, not theirs.

"They're sure. I know the owner, and I promise he'll love your work. And you."

The hitch in her voice brought my hesitation back. Out of four older sisters and my parents, she was the only member of my family who still spoke to me. I'd been *shunned* when the rest of them realized I was bisexual. Brooke was not only okay with it, she was forever trying to *help* me get over Tanner. "Are you trying to set me up?"

"No." She managed to pour a lot of offense into a single syllable. "You'll take care of that on your own when the sparks fly between the two of you."

I plugged my laptop in. "I doubt it, but I'll take the job."

"Awesome. I'll send you his info, and let him know you can start… tomorrow morning?"

"Sounds perfect." After I hung up with her, I finished unpacking enough to be comfortable for the next week, then grabbed my bag to head to the pool.

I changed, rinsed off in the shower, and found

Tanner waiting by the water. He shifted his weight from one foot to the other as I approached.

"You need to take a piss?" I asked when I was within hearing range.

He grinned. "Nope. But you're going to wet yourself when you hear this. I talked to John this morning, and he's selling the building."

I stared blankly at Tanner, not sure what I was supposed to be excited about. It had been hard enough to find this place for us to rent for lessons. "Huzzah?"

"We're going to buy it."

Whoa. "What?"

"Not quite the response I expected." Tanner's smile dropped, but I knew him well enough to recognize the enthusiasm still raged strong. "This is the opportunity we've been waiting for. Sure, it's a little ahead of our schedule, but we're so close to being able to nab the place."

"Unless he's asking a lot less than market value"—which I couldn't imagine—"we can't afford it."

Now Tanner was frowning. "What's with the negativity?"

Realism. But that wasn't the point. "There are tiles missing in the locker rooms, and the HVAC needs some serious work. The rooms in the other building smell like chlorine." This place was supposed to be a full-blown rec center, but John only focused on the pool. "He's selling so he doesn't have to pay to repair it."

"A brand new place would take work too. Construction. Decisions. Here, we know what to expect."

I wasn't sure we did.

"Come on. This is our dream." Tanner tossed the words out that always made me cave.

Voices bounced around the cavernous room as our first students filtered in. This was our youngest class at five to seven years old, so we only allowed six students into the course. We needed to keep an eye on all of them, but I also hated turning new enrollments away. Part of growing would mean hiring more coaches.

"It wouldn't hurt to look more closely into it," I said.

His grin was back. "Wicked."

"Mithter Manthell." The call rang out. The *th* in place of the *s*'s in my name told me who it was, even though the acoustics in here distorted voices.

I turned to see Edward, one of the smaller boys, running toward me, grinning broadly enough to show the gap where his two front teeth were still growing in. I pushed aside my mixed reaction to Tanner's news, and crouched to bring myself to eye level with Edward. "No running near the pool. What's up?" I asked. Someday I'd have kids of my own—I'd always wanted a family—but for now, I was content to teach other people's children.

"I practithed all week. I can do my doggy paddle now." He'd been struggling with that.

"That's fantastic." I moved to the edge of the water and dropped in, gesturing for him to drop in. "Show me."

For the next hour, we worked with the kids on basic strokes, but just as much we let them have fun. Tanner would require structure from anyone who advanced to higher level classes, but for the beginners, I insisted we keep swimming playful rather than a chore.

The news about the building lingered in my head, as well as my mixed feelings. Why wasn't I as excited as Tanner? My life had been a lot of drifting from job to job and interest to interest, and nothing had given me stability except this. I loved what we were doing, and we'd been planning this for so long.

This must be trepidation. The kind of uncertainty that came with a dream becoming more real.

The entire situation stayed on a loop in my thoughts as we wrapped up class, and headed back to Daria's. I arrived a moment before Tanner, hesitated at the door, then reminded myself it was okay to walk inside without knocking. We had keys for a reason.

Daria was in the kitchen, and looked up when I walked in. Her friendly smile melted into furrowed eyebrows when she met my gaze. "What's wrong?"

Did she somehow know I was struggling with uncertainty? Tanner hadn't seemed to notice anything.

"Nothing's wrong." Speaking of… He joined us. "In fact, everything's fucking awesome."

"Oh yeah?" She sounded genuinely curious. Then again, most things she did were genuine. One of the things I liked about her was her sincerity. I liked a lot of things about Daria, though. If I weren't so hung up on Tanner, and she weren't a student's parent, I'd entertain a lot of fantasies about her.

Tanner laid out our opportunity to buy the building.

"That's amazing." She smiled warmly. "My offer still stands if you need help with paperwork or another set of eyes on your business proposal."

The grin Tanner gave her was one of those that always made my heart skip. "We may take you up on that, once you're done with your work crisis."

"You know where to find me." She grabbed her coffee mug, and headed downstairs again.

Tanner turned to me. "I'm sorry if I was abrupt earlier."

"You weren't. This is important, and you're right —we've been planning it for so long."

His grin was back, turning my insides to mush now that it was focused on me. "I'm not going to just dive into this or move forward without due-diligence. And I'm not doing it without you."

The words should've warmed me further, but they added to an unease I still didn't feel I'd identified. "Let's go make plans, then."

4
daria

DAY one of my non-existent vacation was in the bag.

The girls called when they got back to their hotel, and I could see the pink in Harmony's cheeks. I reminded her to have Alana help her with sunscreen tomorrow, then listened while she told me all about her day. About meeting Cinderella and all the rides she went on and how Daddy won her a giant, pink Minnie Mouse.

Her smile and excitement were contagious, and I couldn't help my grin as she told her story. I was grateful there was no *Daddy is a dickhead* included in the tale.

Alana was smiling just as much. She'd gotten to go on the rides. She saw cute boys and Joe hadn't embarrassed her in front of them, and she had a new swim suit for the water park.

I blew them kisses over Facetime, easily squashed

the minuscule bit of disappointment that their dad was showing them a good time while I was stuck working, and wished them both *sweet dreams*.

I should put aside work for the night and relax, but the day's crisis and disappointment had me wound up, even at almost eleven at night. If I put in a little more work, I could finish things early and maybe get the second half of my week off.

There would be no beaches waiting for me as a reward, but a few days of sleeping in, mimosas, and afternoon reading in the sun sounded like an okay substitute. Not great, but I was looking for the positive in all this.

The scenery in my office—four windowless walls and as many cluttered whiteboards—was tired though. I grabbed my laptop and headed up to the living room. A few minutes later, I had a bottle of beer and a bowl of carrots. I made myself comfortable in my favorite corner of the sectional, and tucked my legs under me, feet to the side.

As long as I kept the sound on the TV low, I shouldn't disturb my guests. Lucky for me, Baywatch was on. No sound required. Was I really watching this just for the pretty people running on the beach?

For the most part.

Did I care?

Nope.

I gave my half-hearted attention to my spreadsheets and frequently glanced at the screen, appreciating the hard bodies.

One of the bedroom doors clicked open. It wasn't a loud sound, but I had years of listening for the same with the girls, and their rooms were a floor higher.

Colin wandered out, and we exchanged friendly smiles and nods. He headed into the kitchen and I tried to turn back to my work. But the real life hard body walking away from me made for a much better view. His shorts hung low on his hips, and hinted at the ass underneath.

He stepped to the other side of the island, cutting off part of the view. When he opened the fridge door, back lighting himself, shadows rolled across his arms with the ripple of muscle. He bent to grab something, completely vanishing for a moment, and I took the opportunity to tear my gaze away.

Whew. So pretty to look at, even if both men were hands-off.

"Do you want anything?" His soft call carried toward me.

You. Naked in front of me. We can figure the details out from there. "I'm good, thanks." Except I was apparently a lot horny. I had solutions for that upstairs, though.

Colin wandered back into the living room, bottle of water in hand, and took a seat on the couch, not far from my feet. "You're really dedicated to your work." He sounded more awed than judgmental.

"It pays the bills. Besides, this is the menial stuff to numb my brain so I can sleep."

"Same for the TV show? *There* was the hint of judgement.

I didn't mind. "What? No." I feigned surprise. "I'm watching this for the *plot*."

"Hmm." He furrowed his brow and kept his attention on the TV. "What's the plot of this episode?"

"That guy there, in the red trunks?" I gestured vaguely. "He's got to run into the water and save someone. And then there's some drama. And some more running."

He still hadn't taken his gaze off the screen. "In slow motion even."

"See? You get it."

Colin shook his head with a laugh. "I guess we all have our guilty pleasures."

"I don't feel guilty about this." I felt guilty about not spending enough time with the girls. About poorly balancing home and work. But not about enjoying Baywatch. "I know exactly what I'm watching and why. I'm not ashamed to admit it."

"Fair point." Colin was fixated on the screen again.

A creaking that I both heard and felt greeted me when I rolled my neck. I was getting too old for hunching over my laptop on the couch and trying to work. I reached a hand to the spot where my neck met my shoulder, and rubbed, wincing at the ache that pulsed in the muscle.

"Let me," Colin said.

Before I could decide if it was inappropriate to let him, he had his hands on my shoulders and his thumbs digging into the muscles at the base of my neck. "You're so tight," he said.

I was grateful for my moan at his skilled touch because it kept me from snickering at his words. *God* that felt good. The longer he massaged, the more my tension faded away. I dipped my head forward and let my hair fall around my face.

"You're amazing." The words came out breathier than I intended.

"I have a lot of practice, especially from Tanner's injury."

I'd seen the way he watched Tanner—it was impossible to miss. It was also pretty obvious Tanner had no idea he felt the same way. Clueless men. Good new fantasy, though. My mind liked the idea of watching both of them, either with me or the two of them alone. The way Colin dug his fingers into my skin helped fuel the desire dancing over my skin.

How long was it appropriate to let him keep doing this?

The other bedroom door creaked open. The instant Tanner stepped into the room, Colin's hands dropped away.

Tanner didn't look fazed. "Am I interrupting something?"

"Nope. Nothing at all," Colin's answer came too quickly.

I didn't appreciate that he sounded embarrassed, almost guilty, but I also knew why. Poor guy was going to spend a lot of time miserable if he didn't either tell Tanner how he felt or decide to move on.

5
daria

MY DREAMS WERE FILLED with an odd blend of shadowy, threatening figures, and shadowy, sexy figures.

The sexy dreams woke me up, heat spilling through me and need throbbing between my legs. Now that I was conscious, last night raced back to join it—Colin's skilled fingers on my neck and shoulders. His incredible voice. That spark of want that Tanner would join us instead of breaking up the party.

Bad idea in real life, but perfect in my fantasies.

I made a straight line to my dresser, and the hidden box at the back of the top drawer. I could use my fingers, or the shower head by itself, but I wanted to be filled up by a thick, long cock.

When Joe and I separated, I went out with— fucked—everyone. Words of affirmation were one hundred percent my love language. Praise fed me, and Joe had left me starving. If a guy cupped my face, looked me in the eye, and told me I was smart and funny and pretty, I'd let him stick his dick anywhere.

The experience taught me junk food was amazing in the moment, but ultimately unsatisfying, and I'd swapped out fucking around for a latex, and battery powered assortment of toys. They didn't praise me, but the faceless younger men in my imagination, who may or may not be built like swimmers, would do plenty of that.

I grabbed a small bottle of lube from the top shelf in the medicine cabinet, though I didn't think I'd need it. As I stripped out of the battered, oversized *They Might be Giants* shirt and granny panties I'd slept in, and turned on the water in the shower, the fantasy was already building. It started just like last night—Colin massaging the kinks from my neck.

There was a fold down seat attached to the wall. It was meant for me to sit on while I shaved my legs, but this morning, the smooth surface was perfect for me to suction cup a dildo to. That was the main course though, and I was still enjoying the appetizer.

I stepped under the water and let the heat wash around and through me. In my fantasy of last night, Colin glided his hands lower as he massaged, slipping under my shirt to cup my breasts and tease. I followed a similar path in reality, letting my soapy palms slip along my skin. As I imagined him rolling my nipples between my fingers, I did the same.

When Tanner stepped out of his room, this time Colin didn't pull his hands away. He pinched harder, sending fissures of delight through me to pool in my belly and travel lower.

Tanner grinned. "This looks cozy. Is there room for one more?"

In my mind, I squirmed on the couch in anticipation and nodded. In the shower I glided my fingers between my legs, but didn't part my folds. My skin was hot and slick and I wasn't ready for the fantasy to be over.

Tanner knelt between my legs and stripped off my bottoms, while Colin glided his lips along the back of my neck, never letting up the attention on my breasts.

Tanner kissed up my upper thighs, sucking then nipping enough to make me gasp, before finally gliding his tongue along my pussy. *Fuck* he knew what he was doing. Where to lick, how to hook his fingers just right inside me, and every muffled murmur of *you taste so good* and *God, I love the sounds you make* amplified my arousal.

And then, because it was imaginary, we were magically on the bed in Tanner's guest room. It was a full-sized bed, not meant for two people let alone three, but we didn't care.

Colin felt incredible, buried inside me as I straddled him, and Tanner was just as intensely amazing sliding into my ass from behind.

I needed that sensation of being filled to be real. I lowered myself onto the dildo, biting the inside of my cheek to keep from moaning too loudly as it stretched me out. Fantasy blended with real sensations as I rode the toy, imagining them hammering inside me hard and fast.

I slipped my fingers between my legs to tease my swollen clit. I was so turned on, so embedded in the daydream, that orgasm spilled through me at my touch. This felt so good, I didn't want it to stop. I fucked and fingered myself until another climax crashed over me, and finally slowed to a stop. My breath came in short gasps and my pulse hammered in my ears.

Imaginary-me collapsed on Colin's chest. The guys softened and slid out of me, Colin trailing his fingers through my hair, and Tanner murmuring, "You're so beautiful."

Water sluiced around me, slowly drawing me back to reality, but not taking away the orgasms.

So. Good.

Not the real thing, but I was satisfied with the outcome.

I finished my shower, tiny reminders shivering through me every time my hands drifted between my legs, and forced myself to get out before I spent the whole morning in here.

I wiped the steam from the bathroom mirror, and a flushed reflection stared back at me. The red in my cheeks was as much from the fun daydream and orgasm as it was from the hot water.

My work schedule today was mostly phone calls, emails, and administrative work. I didn't have any video conferences scheduled, and that usually meant

I'd tug my hair into a ponytail, toss on whatever, and be done with it.

But I wanted to feel stunning, even if no one saw me but me. I took the time to dry my hair enough that that natural wave would stay when I worked product into the curls, and grabbed my favorite shade of lipstick—the burgundy color that made me look incredible. The color I hadn't worn since I stopped fucking around.

I opened the tube and a squashed lumpy stump of nothing laughed at me. One of the girls must have gotten to it before me. At least they enjoyed it rather than it going to waste. I'd have to make do with lip gloss and mascara.

My favorite matching bra and panty set—burgundy satin and lace like the non-existent lipstick—came out of retirement. I didn't care that no one else would see it; putting it on made me feel extra sexy.

The entire look was topped off with a blouse that was probably a shade too thin for me to be wearing dark lingerie under it, and the capris I knew for a fact made my ass look good. There was nothing wrong with a pair of amazing mom jeans when they were comfortable and complimentary.

Now to take my gorgeous self and sit in a basement all day where no one would see me. The thought should have been depressing, but it made me laugh.

I opened the bedroom door and pulled up short at

the sight of Tanner, hand frozen in midair as if he'd been about to knock.

His gaze froze too, right on my chest.

Heat flooded my face. "Can I help you?"

He shook his head and forced his attention up, to look me in the eye. "You look incredible."

Fuck me, please? The whimper echoed in my head, and I forced it aside. "Thank you."

"But I bet you have to get to work." He gave a light cough and the mood shattered. Mostly. "I have a last-minute appointment with a loan officer, and I need to be there in an hour. Colin's in the bathroom downstairs getting ready for a mural job. May I use yours?"

"Of course." I stepped aside.

I left him alone in my bedroom, while my apparently-not-sated hormones screamed at me to go back and jump him. Down girl. Fantasies and daydreams were enough for me. Especially when it came to Alana's coaches.

The thought didn't carry as much weight as it had in the past, and I had to force it to repeat like a scratched CD while I started work.

6

colin

I HATED the uneasy feeling in my gut that said Tanner *caught* me last night. Doing what? Shoulder rubs for Daria? Big fucking deal. Nothing I hadn't done for him thousands of times, and that never meant anything.

Or maybe that was the problem. It always meant something to me. The contact and closeness whenever I helped Tanner work out tight muscles. The soft grunts he made. The fact that last night, massaging Daria's neck left that same light, giddy feeling rushing through me.

And I wanted to think when Tanner saw us, a hint of uncertainty and hesitation splashed across his face. But I didn't know if that was true or if I just wanted it to be.

I emerged from my room, ready for work, and was surprised to see Tanner's door open and him not there. Maybe he went to the pool early. Not usually his thing, but he was pushing harder than he should be for the qualifying trials.

My appointment with Deacon wasn't for another hour. If I got there early though, I could grab a coffee on my way there and spend some time checking the place out. I'd skip breakfast, since we were on a budget, but I always had a couple extra bucks for coffee.

At the creak of a door and footsteps on the stairs, I looked up ready with a smile for Daria, and my throat went dry at the sight of Tanner coming down the stairs, hair damp, and wearing his *make an impression* clothes. The shirt that might be a size too small, but it didn't matter because it showed off how incredibly defined his chest and arms were. The slacks that made his ass look amazing. The outfit he'd brought *just in case* that I teased him for thinking he'd need.

Seeing him like this wasn't new, but seeing him come out of Daria's room freshly showered sent an unreasonable wave of assumption and jealousy coursing through me.

"Hey, I'm glad I caught you." His light tone was enough to jerk me back to *you see him every day, chill the fuck out.*

I returned his smile. "What's up?"

"I landed an early appointment with a small business loan officer. He's going to review our business plan and such. It's not an official application, but I should come away with some pointers and an idea of if we're still on the right track."

"That's awesome." My hesitation from yesterday had vanished, and his enthusiasm was infectious this morning.

His grin spread. "It really is. I'll take lots of notes. You free tonight if we need to make changes?"

"Sure."

"Epic. I'll catch you this afternoon." Tanner turned away.

"About last night." The words slipped out before I could stop them, and I winced, hiding the expression before he looked at me.

Tanner raised his brows. "Which part?"

"With Daria." Stop talking. Shut up. But it was too late. Not finishing the thought would make things worse. "There was nothing going on."

Tanner's easy chuckle sliced through me. "I get it. She's fun to hang with, she's smokin' hot, and I don't see her pulling Alana from classes or kicking us out over a neck rub, so it's all good."

"Right. Catch you later."

He waved and headed outside.

I slouched, resting my weight against the counter behind me. Why was I doing this to myself? A hint of pain in the bedroom was fun, but I'd never thought of myself as a masochist. But poking and prodding Tanner day after day to see if he felt more for me than friendship, and continually being let down, was me torturing myself.

Work called, and supposedly I got to design today.

Losing myself in a mural would be the perfect way to reset my mind.

The antique shop was nestled with other small businesses on Main Street of the small town where Brooke lived. It was a bit of a drive to get here, but it wasn't too bad considering how isolated the place felt.

The limited on street parking made it difficult to get a spot near their awning covered entrances. There was plenty of time for a stroll, so I grabbed a spot a few blocks away. I slung my briefcase containing a giant sketchpad over my shoulder, and after a short pause to grab coffee, I stepped through the doors of Deacon's Derelicts and D'art.

That was a lot of Ds, and with any luck, he was the kind of guy who would snicker at that statement as much as I was.

Inside, a corridor of display cases lined an entry-way, and led to the main store. Behind the glass were assorted knickknacks of pop culture memorabilia—a Scooby Doo lunchbox, an A&W glass mug, and an assortment of decorative shaped tins ranging from trains to bears.

When I reached the main shop, a vast space spread out in front of me that defied how big this place should be, based on outside appearances. I'd walked into a TARDIS of a shop, decorated with Ds. What a glorious day.

"Colin?" A deep, rolling voice drew my attention.

I turned to find a man standing a few feet away,

watching me with piercing green eyes, his dirty blond hair pulled into a bun on the top of his head. He was cute. Not drop my coffee to swoon cute, and in the beige tank top and khakis, probably more Brooke's type than mine. "You must be Deacon."

"I'll be whoever you're looking for." He winced as he extended his hand. "That was awful, wasn't it?"

When I shook his hand his grip was firm and warm. I didn't know if I wanted the feeling to do something for me or not, but it didn't. "It wasn't great." I kept my tone light. It would be easy to take the line and run with it. Something like *but it was cute.* I couldn't push out the words, though. "But I've heard a lot worse, so I won't hold it against you," I teased. "I know I'm early, so don't feel like you need to drop everything because I'm here."

"I am *super* busy right now." He cast his gaze around the shop with a faint smile.

The place was full... of furniture, fixtures, art, and I was pretty sure that was a battered shield in the corner next to a spear. But there were no other people. "I can see that."

"I'll make time for you, though." He gestured toward the far wall, which was currently covered with painted recreations of kitsch. Like a sports bar, but not real objects. "I had someone do that about six months ago, I gave them artistic freedom and they gave me Coca-Cola logos. According to Brooke, you can do better."

"I can do different. Better is a matter of opinion. But yeah, I can do better."

"I'm already sold. How does this work? Do you keep your paints in your magic sack?"

I shook my head with a smile. "I'll sketch out a concept, if you like what you see, there's a fifty percent deposit"—which would pay for the paints, so I wasn't out that cost if for some reason a client didn't finish paying—"and I start work tomorrow."

"And I get to watch you work?"

Heat flooded my face. The blatant flirting was nice, but I didn't know how to rebuff it politely. Why couldn't I get this from Tanner?

Why was I so hung up on him? After all this time, he wasn't going to see me as more than a friend, and I wasn't going to push the issue. If I could move on, so many more opportunities would open up for me. Someone like Deacon. Hell, even someone like Daria —sweet, funny, a fantastic mom whose kids I adored….

That was it, I was done swooning over Tanner. Obviously easier said than done, but I was cutting myself off from the fantasy. It wasn't doing me or him or our friendship any favors, and it was certainly hurting my dating life.

7

tanner

I WAS USED to hearing *yes*, so I was confident about this morning's meeting.

But the entire drive to the bank, rather than staying focused on the facts of our business proposal, my mind bounced between two distractions. Seeing a bottle of lube near the bathroom sink and that dildo in Daria's shower, suction cupped in place, still glistening with drops of water, had me picturing her riding it. Riding me.

And she was flushed and smiling shyly in my fantasy, exactly the way she had when I talked to her in the doorway.

I pushed the thought aside as best I could. Walking into an appointment with a hardon made a supremely bad impression.

Which was when Colin slid into my head, carried on last night, and the associated whisper that I wouldn't have minded being a part of whatever I'd walked in on, and making it more. With her. Hell, even with him there.

And that left me thinking about Colin. Kind, thoughtful, brilliant, bizarrely single despite having double the options open to him...

He'd been off since we got to Daria's and I didn't know why. He was more than a roommate or best friend or business partner—Colin was my anchor. He'd helped me through my injury and I could always count on him. I wouldn't want to go into this venture without him.

When I was done here, I'd do something to cheer him up, and get him to tell me what was wrong.

I pulled into the bank parking lot, and a lifetime of training for the public eye kicked in. I wiped any other thoughts from my mind like sweeping off a table to use it for fuc—

Nope. I was focused on the meeting.

The woman working the front desk gave me a broad smile and leaned in as I approached. "May I help you?"

I could flirt. Get her number. But I couldn't stop thinking about someone a little older who I already knew was great company. "Tanner Hagen. I have an appointment with Mr. Davenport."

"From the Olympics?" Her face lit up brighter.

Not for a while, but I would be again. "That's me."

"We watched you in gym class, sophomore year. I felt so bad when you got hurt."

"Thanks. Can I go up?"

"I'll let Mr. Davenport know you're here."

I kept my smile in place, but something inside wilted. I wouldn't do the math to figure out how much younger that made her. Did Daria feel like this talking to me?

And what was my hang-up today? So I saw her dildo, and now I couldn't get her out of my head? Maybe today was the perfect day to indulge a fantasy and hook up with her. Get the urge out of my system, and see what that dark bra looked like when I stripped her top off...

"Mr. Davenport will see you." The receptionist interrupted my wandering thoughts.

Which was good. I stood, told my dick *down boy*, and headed toward his office.

I'd talked to Davenport a couple of times already. He was part of a program that offered free consultation to small business owners and start-ups. The option to buy an existing building changed so many things. I wanted to get his opinion on the deal, and since he worked for one of the local banks, I was hoping to catch his eye and have him offer to move to the next steps of the loan process. Or at least give me a referral to a colleague.

He greeted me with a handshake, we chatted about the weather for a few minutes, and then I launched into my pitch.

The basics hadn't changed much. We currently taught swimming lessons to kids from five to eighteen, and we wanted to expand our operations. Bring on more coaches, put ourselves in a building we owned, that provided a place for families to swim when classes weren't in session, and even provide more adult classes like water aerobics.

I pointed to profit and loss history and projections. Experience. The power of my name as a brand and a selling point...

"And we always come back to the same thing," he said. "You need a large chunk of land and a lot of money to build something like this. You said the situation had changed?"

"It has." I'd printed the real estate listing for the building we were in now, grabbed specs, floor plans, and everything I could think of. I flipped to that new information now. "We have the opportunity to purchase an existing structure."

Davenport's brows knitted together.

That wasn't right.

"I'm familiar with the property." His cheer vanished behind a flat tone. "More specifically, I'm familiar with the disrepair most of it is in."

My enthusiasm dipped a notch, but I didn't let the reaction show. "Nothing structural, though." I hoped. Please don't let the place have the kind of issues that would require tearing it down. "I realize it needs more than a fresh coat of paint"—I flipped to another new section of the plan—"but you'll see here we also have plans to renovate the rest of the building. Bring the classrooms back up, the gym, and put other activities in place."

Colin had some brilliant ideas around restoration and rebuilding. He'd even provided some preliminary sketches. One of the best things about talking to him about this part of the plan was the way his face lit up when he went into detail about what he'd do, given the chance. Colin inspired and embracing his muse was a beautiful sight.

Davenport placed his hand on the pages of my business proposal before I could flip to Colin's concepts. "Managing and maintaining a rec center is a very different idea than running a swim school and pool. You were already looking at costly insurance, utilities, and upkeep. This adds new layers to all of it."

"I understand that, but—"

"Do you?" He met my gaze and held it. "I appreciate what you're trying to do and why. You've put together a fantastic business plan since we started speaking. However, with these new ideas you can't just slap a few pages in the middle of your proposal and call it done. Especially when you're looking at a dilapidated piece of property that no bank is going to give you a loan for."

I didn't appreciate being cut off or talked down to. "You're missing the vast opportunity here."

"I assure you, I'm not." He stood. "Take some time to think about what I've said." He stepped around the desk, to the door, and held it open. "And enjoy the rest of your day."

What just happened? "I'll rework the proposal to

include the rec center, and we'll talk again in a week or so." I stood and gathered my things, but I wasn't leaving on this note. "Should I schedule with the girl up front or drop you an email?"

Davenport shook his head. "Lose this building and-slash-or come back with fifty percent down, and you'll find a lot of doors open up. Regardless, lose the rec center idea."

My thoughts were stuck in a loop. I didn't know how to deal with the brush off, and I wanted to argue and tell him how wrong he was. However, I refused to let him see me upset or give the impression of begging. "Thank you for your time. I won't be scheduling future meetings."

"I understand."

I didn't. As I walked back to the parking lot, I tried to figure out how any of this made sense. My idea, the proposal, was brilliant. His point about updating the P&L was a good one, but nothing else he'd said rang true.

I climbed into my car, disbelief spinning toward anger. It was time to stop piddling around with consultations from a man who was looking for reasons to say *no*. A few tweaks this afternoon, and I was going directly to bankers. Fuck him and his bullshit brush-off.

Next steps spun through my head as I headed back to Daria's. I'd let Colin go full-force on redesign ideas. We'd make this entire concept leap off the page.

This route was unfamiliar, and as I drove, I

vaguely registered the new scenery. Mostly small local places I hadn't seen before that looked like I might want to visit later. A sign with a stunning hand-painted script caught my eye. It was advertising high end drawing pens on clearance.

Colin had been eyeing those for a long time, putting it off because we were being frugal. I made a hard right into the parking lot, and a short while later emerged with the new gift in hand. The pens weren't as cheap as I'd hoped, but I could suck it up financially for a few weeks. Seeing him smile would be worth it.

Plus, if he didn't know this place was here, I'd need to bring him by.

Excitement at the idea of brightening Colin's day blended strangely with my frustration, and by the time I parked in Daria's driveway, unspent energy thrummed inside, screaming for a physical outlet.

I could head back to the pool, but I wasn't in the mood to spend more time in the car first. I could throw on a pair of shorts and go for a run.

The light clang of dishes caught my attention as I walked through the front door, and I followed the noise to find Daria in the kitchen. Her back was to me, and her dark hair fell in loose waves around her shoulders, begging to be pulled...

New plan. I'd engage her help to burn off this excess adrenaline. "Lunchtime?"

She jumped and whirled to face me. "Fuck, you startled me." Her shaky laugh was the perfect complement to the pink spreading across her cheeks. "And yes, I was thinking about it."

"Not sure if you have something specific in mind, but I have a suggestion for something delicious if you'd like some company."

"What are you thinking?" Daria asked.

"You."

Her snort-laugh, and the way she cut it off by clamping her mouth shut, was the last response I expected.

Sure, I'd come on a bit strong, but direct tended to be the best way to let someone know *Hey, I'd like to fuck you.* "There's no way I'm that unappealing." I kept my tone light.

Her smile was shy and she didn't meet my gaze. "It's not... You're not... I'm sorry." She looked up. "The laugh was more of an *I didn't expect that* noise. I was leaning toward grilled cheese if you'd like one too."

Smoothest brush-off ever. At least she didn't offer me a PB&J with the crust cut off.

Was it wrong that I thought it was sexy that her default for food was making traditionally for-kids food? Hell, the fact that she was such a great parent in general was sexy. "Grilled cheese sounds great."

Sure, she'd brushed me off, and changed the topic so quickly she never missed a beat, but I hadn't been shut down.

Still, my ego limped along, not sure what to make of the day of *nos*.

8

daria

I PROBABLY SHOULDN'T HAVE LAUGHED when Tanner propositioned me. His approach was smoother than anything my imagination would've come up with.

It was also way too *cheesy porn* for me to take it seriously.

I couldn't bring myself to say *yes*, but I also didn't want to tell him *no* and completely remove the option. The line was bad, but I liked being called *delicious* and he was yummier in person than in my fantasies. Basically, I didn't want to completely discourage him.

So, being the dork I was, I'd offered him a sandwich instead. Go me. I wanted to pretend this was no big deal, but it was easier to focus on the cooking than looking at Tanner or trying to make conversation.

"Can I help with anything?" He hadn't left. That had to be a good sign.

The offer was kind. The thought of working shoulder to shoulder with him heated my skin. "You can load the dishwasher after, but I've got it, thanks." Besides, I had this down to a science. Heat the electric griddle while I got out the supplies. Mayo on the outside of the bread, cheese in the middle, drop two sandwiches on right as the surface was the right temperature.

Easy peasy.

"How did things go at the bank?" I asked as the food cooked.

"Not great. Not yet."

A corner of my mouth tugged up at the confidence. That was sexy. "Yet?"

"It wasn't a *no* and I'm willing to modify my proposal for a *yes*."

He was still talking about the bank, wasn't he? Or was he talking about me?

Nah.

When I glanced over my shoulder, he pulled his gaze up from where it would've been focused on my ass, and grinned.

Maybe he was talking about me. The flutters in my stomach liked that idea.

"Give me details. You can't drop a vague answer like that and then just leave it." I was talking about the business proposal, but I wouldn't mind if he interpreted my words differently.

"The building's not in the best shape, and the business plan doesn't allow for some of the new costs involved, but Colin has some great ideas, and I can revise the budget."

Business it was, then. I didn't have a right to be disappointed—I brought it on. I dished the sandwiches onto two plates, cut them in half diagonally, and set the food on the counter dividing the kitchen from the dining room. One dish in front of Tanner and the stool he sat on, and one for me.

"Do you want to sit?" he asked.

The thought hadn't even occurred to me. "Actually, I have to get back to work." I didn't want to. Especially with this sexy guy watching me with rapt attention, and the potential for the conversation to get playful again, but I hadn't intended to walk away from my desk for long.

"I get it." Disappointment whispered through Tanner's reply. "Don't work too hard, and thanks for lunch."

I gave him a faint smile, grabbed my food, and headed back to my *dungeon* under the house.

What would've happened if I'd said *okay* when he said he wanted me for lunch? We'd probably be fucking right now. The visuals played off my fantasy from this morning, splashing a whole new layer of vibrance and heat across the images in my mind.

As I settled at my desk, Colin flitted back into my thoughts. In a sexy, let's-have-a-threesome kind of way, but also in a he-was-completely-obsessed-with-Tanner kind of way. Colin's reaction last night, when Tanner saw him giving me a neck rub, was the strongest evidence I'd seen yet, but the attraction was anything but subtle.

I was also pretty sure it didn't go both ways. At least, not that Tanner had admitted to himself.

Which wouldn't stop me from feeling guilty if I hooked up with Tanner. Yeah, I was pretty sure he fucked around a lot, and that Colin expected it, but I doubted any of those women knew what kind of relationship they had.

Sometimes being able to get an intuitive read on people sucked.

I nibbled on my sandwich and dove back into work, firing off an email to one of the senior partners asking for additional information, then turning to the next item on my to-do list.

My phone rang, and the name *Kandace Newton* flashed on screen. The woman I'd just reached out to.

"This is Daria." I slid into my sweet-but-take-no-shit professional voice without pause.

"It certainly is. I'd hoped when I saw your name in my inbox it was a fluke. What the hell are you doing working?" Kandace's tone was light, despite the admonishment. "You're supposed to be in Hawaii."

I swallowed my sigh at the reminder. Hawaii would be so much less complicated. Fresh memories of Colin and Tanner, both shirtless and dripping wet from climbing out of the pool, popped into my head.

The company may not be as good somewhere else, though.

"Last minute client emergency," I said. "My plans were already off-kilter, so I said yes."

Her *hmm* sounded a bit like a growl. "Bernie?"

I didn't want to sic the senior partners on each other but lying or ignoring the question wasn't smart either. "Yes."

She clucked. "Ridiculous. Finish your day and take the rest of the week off. This is your vacation."

"But—" I clenched my jaw. I appreciated the sentiment, but I also had work to do now that I was here.

"That's an order. I'll take care of him, and you'll get paid whatever he promised you. Understand?"

I almost smiled at her stern tone. "Yes."

"Good. I'll send you over the information you're asking for, but don't let me hear a peep from you after today. Not until next Monday."

How was I supposed to argue with that? "Understood."

I turned my attention to my laptop.

What if I could nudge Colin and Tanner together?

The question came out of nowhere and now that it was in my head, I didn't want to ignore it.

Not as in just the two of them. Not at first. More like, I could have my sexy threesome and they could have a taste of each other at the same time I did.

A hookup like that could be bad for a friendship. I was horrible for even considering it beyond a fantasy level. I mean... unless all three of us agreed it was no big deal.

It would be for Colin, no matter what. I couldn't pretend otherwise.

But what if it became more for Tanner, too? He

had stories from the Olympic campus of threesomes. Of rampant fucking and basically orgies. Not the kind of thing he shared during class, but he'd boasted more than once when only the adults were around.

I tried to push the idea aside, but it lingered through the rest of the workday, still teasing and tempting me as I set my *Out of Office* notifications and shut everything down.

My phone rang, FaceTime from the girls. Hearing from them made me smile, but getting the call so early in the day made me suspicious.

They were still having a blast though. Harmony needed to be wearing more sunscreen, based on how pink her cheeks were, but they were both excited for dinner with Mickey tonight. I blew them kisses, sent them on their way, and headed upstairs.

When I reached the main floor, Tanner was in the dining room, laptop in front of him, typing away.

Hey, what if all three of us fucked? The question bounced in my thoughts.

No way was I saying that. "I'm getting a beer, do you want one?" I headed for the fridge and grabbed two bottles.

"Not apple juice in a sippy cup?" Tanner's teasing question hit my back.

I pressed cold glass to the inside of my wrist to sap away some of the heat flooding me. Nope, didn't work. I took a seat next to him at the table instead, and slid him one of the bottles. "If that's your kink..."

"My kink is making a gorgeous woman scream in

the bedroom." He closed his laptop, took the bottle opener from me, and popped the top on both drinks.

God in heaven help me. It was such a cocky response, and the way he delivered it with zero hesitation had my pulse racing. I took a long swallow of my beer, measuring my reply. "Let's be honest, that's most men's kink."

"Not from what I've heard." He smirked. "It's my understanding a lot of guys are only focused on getting themselves in, off, and out."

"Touché."

"What makes you scream in the bedroom?" He didn't miss a beat, did he?

And I wasn't a doe-eyed fangirl in a bar, no matter how much my body was reacting to the fact his arm settled next to mine, sending heat spilling between us. Attraction and fantasy were nice, but the stubborn part of me wasn't doing this—whatever *this* was—unless I was fully convinced. "Dirty socks on the floor directly next to the clothes hamper."

"Fair point." His smirk became a chuckle. "But seriously for a moment."

This was fun. How was this fun? "I'll try."

"Your actual kink?"

My response stuck in my throat as I wavered between giving him a version of the truth and tugging up another diversionary response.

"Long work hours. Never slowing down. I bet you're a masochist," Tanner said.

"Nope." I popped the *p*. "To each their own, but

for me, there's enough pain in the world already. A little light spanking and hair pulling is the extent of the sting I'm looking for. I want to be pampered in the bedroom. You?"

He glided his fingers lightly along the back of my neck and I couldn't suppress my gasp at the shudder of desire his touch elicited.

"Wrapping a woman's hair around my fingers"— he knotted his hand lightly in my curls—"looking her in the eye"—he held my gaze—"and telling you what a gorgeous girl you are while I glide my cock into your mouth."

My breath caught and my anticipation spiked. I stopped the *yes please* from whimpering past my lips. "That's only sexy depending on what comes before and after." The shift in pronouns hadn't escaped me either.

"Before? You. After? You again, but hopefully both of us." Tanner let go of my hair, brushing his fingers over my cheek as his hand fell back to the table.

Part of me was fully aware he could be saying whatever it took to get me into bed. A much louder part was absolutely into and turned on by this conversation. "The *you* in this case being a singular and unspecified entity."

"The *you* in this case being *you*." His gaze never left mine.

This wasn't working. Sure, the attention was amazing, and yes, my body was begging for what he was offering, but I couldn't make myself suspend disbelief. I wrapped my hands around my beer, to keep myself from fidgeting. "Where is this coming from?"

"I don't understand."

That was my line. I didn't understand what either of us was doing. "Don't take my question the wrong way, you talk a good game. But... it came out of nowhere." There it was—the root of my biggest hesitation. I got along great with both guys, trusted them, it was why they were in my home. And yes, I'd drooled and fantasized and probably—definitely—lightly flirted on more than one occasion. Especially with Tanner; he made it easy.

But this? It was as if someone had flipped Tanner's *horny* switch and he homed in on the nearest body.

He raked his fingers through his hair and exhaled noisily.

Damn it, that flash of insecurity made him even more attractive. But I still wanted an answer.

The familiar sound of the deadbolt on the front door unlocking made my heart seize, and Colin walked in.

All my curiosity about threesomes rushed back, carrying my reservations about coming between Colin and Tanner along with it.

9
colin

THE HOUSE WAS QUIET. This time of the evening was Daria still working? She'd looked so good doing so last night on the couch. Relaxed. Those soft moans.

It needed to be okay for me to look at others that way who weren't Tanner. To admit I was attracted to other people. Maybe not a student's parent and our temporary landlord, but I really couldn't think of a better starting point.

I headed toward the basement, startled to find Daria and Tanner sitting at the kitchen table, not saying anything and not doing much of anything either.

"Did I interrupt something?" This was awkward.

"I was just asking when you both ate, and if now was too early." Did Daria's voice just waver?

I pulled out a chair and made myself comfortable. "Don't stop on my account. Hell, mind if I watch?" What was I doing? Deciding not to fixate on

Tanner didn't mean it was a good time to channel him.

"I don't usually do things for an audience, but there's a first time for everything," Daria said.

Tanner grinned. "I do everything for an audience." Despite the expression, his voice was missing a lilt.

"When you say eating, you're being literal, not metaphorical?" Oh, God. Did I really just say that? I'd been watching Tanner *way* too long. "You know what, I'm done. I must have picked up some attitude at work." I laughed, hoping to take the edge off my temporary weirdness.

"*I* was being literal." Did Daria relax when she spoke? "We plan meals around our schedules, so I don't remember when normal people have dinner anymore."

"Whenever." I shrugged.

She glanced at Tanner, who made a similar gesture.

He'd gone quiet fast. What did I actually walk into?

"I was thinking Chinese. What do you both like?" Daria grabbed her phone. "It's on me, so no excuses."

"We can't let you—"

She held up a hand, silencing me. "No excuses. Sweet and sour? Pot stickers? Noodles?"

"Schezwan beef, sesame chicken, ham fried rice." Tanner was back.

Or I'd imagined his silence as being anything other than there. "He nailed it," I said.

Daria placed the order and disconnected.

"Oh." Tanner shot up from his seat as if he'd been shocked. He pointed at me. "Don't go anywhere. I'll be right back."

"And I was going to run out to the moon," I teased. What did that even mean?

Daria's laugh was light and natural. She was really pretty when she was relaxed. She was pretty regardless, but this was a side of her I rarely saw. What else had I been missing by focusing so much on Tanner?

"Here." Tanner set a rectangle wrapped in several plastic bags in front of me, and took his seat again. "Happy unbirthday. No give backs." His easy smirk was back.

Not that I was paying that much attention. The shape and rattle of the present were familiar, but there was no way. I unwrapped the gift, my heart sinking and soaring simultaneously when I saw a familiar logo. It was really the hundreds of dollars pen set I'd been eyeing for ages. "I—"

"Shh…" Tanner pressed a finger to my lips. "Unless you're about to say *thank you* or *these are the wrong ones* —which they're not—I don't want to hear it."

I smiled and pulled away from his touch before it could scorch my soul. I could argue cost, ask what the occasion was, or half a dozen other things, but sometimes Tanner did random things like this, and he knew his budget. "They're perfect, thank you."

Was it just me or was this a little awkward? The

three of us sitting around the table, staring at our fingers. I grabbed Tanner's beer and took a long drag off the bottle. Still cold. "Oh, this is good." I pulled it back to check the label. "Strawberry ale?"

"I'm a girl drink drunk." Daria grinned. "If I have to keep beer in the fridge, it needs not taste like old socks."

"Do you? Have to, I mean," I asked.

Daria furrowed her brows. "No one's forcing me to, but I had some left over from a cookout a few weeks ago, and tonight seemed like a good night to finish it off. There's one bottle left if you want it."

"I'm good, thanks." It was tempting to drink a little, loosen up a little, and just let go, but one beer plus Chinese food wouldn't do that, and if it did, the last thing I needed tonight was a reason to question my resolve to relegate Tanner to *friends for life* column. Yup, I was friend-zoning myself.

The small talk bounced from Tanner's time trials to Daria suddenly having the rest of the week off, and even paused on my day, but I was so focused on not paying attention to Tanner, that most of the conversation floated past me.

Pretty sure there was a parallel between that and the last however long of my life.

As we finished eating, Daria started to gather plates and close up boxes.

I grabbed her wrist loosely. "We've got this."

She frowned. "Got what?"

"Go sit on the couch, relax, and we'll clean up," I said.

Daria didn't move, and her disbelief was both tangible and cute.

I didn't suspect she was used to help without having to bribe someone. "I promise you, Tanner knows how to load a dishwasher and I'm perfectly capable of putting leftovers in the fridge. If we weren't capable of taking care of ourselves, our apartment would be a wreck."

She pushed back from the table with an exaggerated sigh. "All right. I will stow my skepticism in favor of your generous offer. Be careful though."

"With...?" I expected her to come back with some quirk about putting things away.

She finally smiled. "A woman could get used to this kind of treatment."

I wished I could promise her that was an option. "Go."

Tanner and I set to work with after-dinner cleanup. Each time one of us brushed past the other in the kitchen, a jolt raced through me. We had far less space at home, and even nursing a crush, this had never been a problem for me before. We were constantly sliding past each other, bumping gently against each other, and placing a casual hand here or there to keep from running into each other.

None of it had ever registered for me the way it did now, when I was trying so hard to ignore any connection we had.

"Are you all right?" Tanner asked quietly. "You seem a little, I don't know, off?"

"I'm fine." My assurance came quickly, and I heard the lie in my tone as much as I tasted it.

Tanner's frown said he didn't buy it any more than I did, but he didn't push the issue.

We finished up, and headed toward the living room, Tanner grabbing the small box with fortune cookies as we walked.

"Heads-up," he said, and tossed a pre-packaged cookie in Daria's direction.

She snagged it out of the air without pause, from her spot on the corner of the sectional. Tanner tossed her a second one, and she caught it easily as well.

He settled in the middle of the couch, and I took a seat at the other end, as far from him as was possible without sitting on the floor. He gave me a questioning look, then tossed me two cookies.

"Ooh, are we playing *in bed*?" Daria asked.

Tanner worked his jaw.

I had no idea how to answer the seemingly nonsensical question. "We're sitting on the couch. Playing what?"

Daria rolled her eyes, the corners of her mouth quirking up. "Where you read the fortune, and add *in bed* to the end."

I didn't get it. I exchanged looks with Tanner, and he shrugged.

"You've never done that." Disbelief filled Daria's question.

I shook my head.

"Time to expand your horizons." Daria cracked her cookie in the package, opened the plastic, and pulled out the slip of paper. "Your road to glory will be rocky, but fulfilling. In bed." She looked up at us, expectation written on her face.

I chuckled. "Okay. I can see the fun in this." I cracked a cookie open and grabbed the fortune. "Courage is not the absence of fear; it is the conquest of it. In bed."

"Yeah, all right, I like this." Tanner laughed. "All things are difficult before they are easy. In bed."

Daria grinned. "That's the truth." She held up her second cookie. "I assume we do two rounds of this?"

"I mean, they gave us six cookies," Tanner said. "It's bad luck not to read the fortunes and read the cookies on the day you get them."

It was a silly superstition, but I'd always found it endearing.

Daria cracked her second cookie open in response, and read aloud. "If you want the rainbow, you have to tolerate the rain. In bed." She wrinkled her nose, but her amusement didn't vanish. "Not sure I'm into that."

"You're not sure?" Tanner asked.

She twisted her mouth and stared at him. "Correction. I'm definitely not into that. Unless we're talking real rain, but not in bed. More like kisses in the rain…" She cleared her throat. "Anyway, Colin's up."

She looked so adorable—flushed and having fun.

No wonder Tanner was spending so much time watching her tonight.

I retrieved my fortune. "The best way to get rid of an enemy is to make a friend. In bed. If orgasms are involved, I could totally see that."

"The right orgasm would make an eternal friend out of me," Daria said. "But it would have to be one hell of an orgasm."

"I'll keep that in mind." Did Tanner's voice just drop an octave?

My jealousy surged, and I swallowed it. "Your turn."

Tanner cracked open the last cookie. "Be passionate and totally worth the chaos. In bed. Truer words were never spoken."

"And I assume few things are more chaotic in bed than adding extra people." Why the fuck did I say that?

Tanner nodded. "True. True."

Daria pursed her lips and raised her brows. "Done that a lot, have you? Added extra people *in bed*?"

"A few times." Tanner was unfazed.

I'd heard these stories and wasn't in the mood to listen again, but I brought up the topic and Daria looked curious. "As long as there's no inappropriate touching, am I right?" I was just setting myself up for a hard fall.

Daria leaned in, elbows on her knees, pressing her breasts together and giving me a view I definitely shouldn't be staring at and absolutely couldn't pull my gaze from. "Beyond consent, where do you draw an *appropriate* line in an orgy?" she asked.

"I didn't participate in the orgies, and when we're talking threesomes, if there's another guy there it's because she wanted it, and that's fine. I'm there for her." Of course he was. Good old Tanner, the ladies' man.

"In other words, *inappropriate* means no making out with the other guy." I tried so hard to keep the bitterness from my voice.

Daria's wince told me I hadn't succeeded. "Wait," she said. "You're telling me all that fucking, and it was one-hundred percent straight affair for you. You've never even kissed another man."

I didn't want to hear his answer, because as much as I wanted to pretend I didn't care, it would hurt more to know he'd experimented with another guy than believing he'd never considered it.

Tanner shook his head. "Balls touch in a three-some"—he said it as casually as *do you need milk from the store*—"but no, never with another guy. Not even kissing."

Thank God.

Daria clucked. "I just… Okay, I guess."

"Why do you seem so surprised?" Tanner asked.

She shrugged. "I figure that's your chance to taste it all, why would you pass it up?"

"Would *you* take the chance for a taste of every-thing?" I was curious.

Daria nodded. "Yes."

"Men. Women?" Now Tanner was the one who sounded skeptical.

"Yes," Daria repeated.

Tanner's eyes grew wide. "You're bi?"

She laughed lightly. "Feeling a bit like a broken record—that's a large vinyl plate with grooves in it, by the way—and yes."

"We know what a record is." And now I liked her even more.

"No way to tell who knows what these days. *Really*, Tanner?" She leaned into the question. "Never even tempted once? All that hot, sexy meat, and no guy even turned your head."

I swore Tanner glanced at me.

"Not a single man in the Olympic village made me want to kiss him," Tanner said.

"I'm just saying you should try it at least once." Daria wasn't leaving this alone. What was her deal?

I didn't want to be doing this; it was time to end the conversation.

Tanner stared at her, brow furrowed. "I should just walk up to some random guy and say "Hey, kiss me so I can see what it's like."

"You'd do it with a woman. Maybe with a line like *you look delicious enough to have for lunch*."

Tanner coughed. "Not again."

"Besides," Daria said. "You don't have to do it with a random stranger. You know a guy who'd help you out so you could say you've done it. Come on. Make tonight a night of firsts."

Lord kill me now. Why couldn't I find my voice to stop this ridiculous conversation?

"Oh my God. Are you trying to get us to kiss?" Tanner sounded scandalized, but not as bothered as I feared. Not really bothered at all.

"What?" Daria held Tanner's gaze. "I practically heard you get an erection when I said I'd been with other women."

I was terrified by every next sentence in this conversation, but now I was fascinated as well. And more hopeful than I wanted to be. I was supposed to be getting over Tanner. "This all seems like a bad idea. We're roommates. Business partners. Best friends."

"True." Daria chewed her bottom lip as she turned her attention to me. "I'd never want to see your friendship damaged. The two of you really are great together."

As friends. Yes. I got it.

Tanner had gone strangely quiet.

Fuck it. I was getting this out of the way so I could move on—so we all could. I stood, tugged Tanner to his feet, and did something I'd wanted to do for more than a decade: I crushed my mouth to his.

Tanner froze, his lips firm and unyielding against mine.

My gut twisted in on itself. What was I doing?

And then Tanner moved his hand to the back of my neck, gripped hard, and leaned into the kiss. He took control, nipping my lip, twisting my heart, tangling his tongue with mine. His body pressed closer, and his erection dug into my pelvis. He tasted like fortune cookies and broken hearts.

I couldn't catch my breath. This was... I'd died and gone to heaven.

When he broke away, his breath came in jagged gasps and his gaze was frozen on mine.

What was I supposed to do now?

I couldn't take it. He wasn't going to reject me. Not after that. "There you go. Now you can say you've done it."

"Yeah. Now I can." Tanner's voice was gravel.

And I needed to keep myself from plummeting into fantasy. "I want to know more about these balls touching threesomes. I mean... three-person sex... Does it really work?"

Tanner shook his head hard enough to rattle something loose. "Depends on the group." He still sounded husky. "There are times a person gets left out, but if everyone is into it..."

I assumed it worked sometimes. Alana talked about how her uncle Dustin had both a boyfriend and a girlfriend, but the last thing I was doing was bringing up students or kids or brothers. I was rock hard from that kiss, and my imagination was running rampant with fantasies of what came next.

Except, Tanner wasn't the only other person naked and kissing me in my imagination. The way Daria watched us now, face flushed, dark bra peeking through pale cotton, and top unbuttoned enough to hint at round, firm breasts, had her joining us in my imagination.

"Is there any way to know if everyone's into it before you start?" I asked.

Daria's smile was both shy and seductive. "It does seem to be a night of experimentation. I'd be into it."

Wait. I'd gone from being surprised and relieved that Tanner had never been with another man, to kissing, to talking about all three of us...

Seriously?

Whatever kind of weird, amazing alternate dimension I'd stepped into, I wanted to stay here as long as possible.

10
daria

WATCHING Colin and Tanner kiss may have been the single hottest thing I'd ever witnessed. They had fireworks on the Fourth of July levels of sparks, and if Colin was into this idea of all three of us, I didn't want to come up with any excuses to turn them both down.

"How does this work?" I asked.

"How does any sex work? Very first it helps if you're close enough to each other to touch." Tanner grasped my fingers, tugged me to my feet, and pulled me closer to him and Colin. "From there, it's also nice to have a space big enough for three people, and then we see where the night takes us."

Sounded simple enough. Once we got to figuring out where limbs went and which pegs went in which holes, I assumed things would get more complicated, but I could start with simple. "So... my room?"

The heat and anticipation pulsing through me

made it easy to ignore how very unsexy the train of all three of us traipsing up the stairs was.

We stepped into my room, and a strange shiver passed through me. I didn't bring one-night stands home, and I hadn't seen anyone more significant since the divorce.

"You all right?" Colin asked.

This definitely fell into the *one-night stand* category, but it wasn't as though we were going to accidentally run into the girls. I pushed the thought aside and smiled. "Now we see where the night takes us, huh?"

"That's what I hear." Colin cupped my face between his palms and kissed so very gently. His hesitation made my heart skip, and when he pressed in harder with a groan, I gasped. Heat and desire spilled inside as we devoured each other in a hungry kiss. I gripped his shirt in my fists, needing something —anything—to keep me grounded.

This wasn't confident, *I do this all the time,* this was the desperation mixed with uncertainty and stolen kisses that needed to be all consuming before they came to an end at curfew. I hadn't been kissed like this since college. A whimper rose in my throat and I swallowed the sound.

Tanner brushed his lips along my neck. "There's no one here but us," he murmured. "You don't have to be quiet."

I hadn't even considered that. Silence and orgasms went hand in hand at home.

Tanner tugged my hair hard enough to draw a

surprised groan from me as he pulled me away from Colin. Tanner yanked my head back and hovered his mouth over mine. "Good girl."

The angle was odd, but the praise was delicious and his kiss was intoxication made more intense by the fact that I was pressed between two hard bodies.

God, this felt amazing, and we'd only rounded first base.

Colin trailed his fingers down the center of my chest, undoing the buttons on my shirt along the way, and letting the fabric hang loose when he reached the bottom. When he pressed back in, his shirt, his jeans, and his erection pressed into my bare stomach, tempting me with the contrast in textures and topography. He glided his palms up my sides with a feather-light touch, adding to the simmer, and drew my chin back for another kiss.

Tanner unhooked my bra with a flick of efficiency, and the tension vanished around my chest. He lifted the lace out of the way.

The cool air against my breasts vanished in a blanket of warmth when his hands moved in, to knead gently. How was this happening? If one of them pinched me, would I wake up? I wasn't willing to risk it.

Tanner pressed his lips to the hollow behind my ear. "I loved that groan," he murmured. "What will it take to get more from you?"

I could be coy, say something like *I'm sure you'll*

figure it out, but asking for what I wanted tended to yield the best success. "Suck on my nipples."

"Fuck, I like the way you say that." Tanner honed in his focus, rolling one hard nub between his fingers, as Colin dropped his head and wrapped his lips around the other.

At the shock of wet heat and suction, I gasped and pressed into Colin's mouth. I made sure to let out every whimper and sigh as Colin devoured and Tanner caressed.

Need pulsed between my thighs and I squeezed my legs together. It didn't help to either diminish or feed the desire. I'd heard some women could get off this way, just by having their breasts played with. I wasn't one of them, but it was tempting to let the men try a little longer.

I covered Tanner's hand, and guided it away from my breast and down my stomach, to press into my mound. His *mmm* rumbled through my back as he undid my jeans and slid his hand under my panties.

"So wet." He slipped his fingers along my skin. "Fucking incredible." He dipped between my folds.

The delicious shock of his touch penetrated a layer of anticipation. I grunted and my hips bucked to get closer. I needed something to hold onto. Some way to reciprocate, but I couldn't reach Tanner. I cupped Colin's cock through his jeans.

He jerked into me with a laugh that ended in a groan. I stroked him while Tanner did the same to me.

"I want to hear you come. Again and again."

Tanner dipped toward my opening then back up to my clit. "Show me what you like."

I covered his hand again, pressing my fingers over his and into my aching need. He let me set the rhythm and pressure, and I liked this too much to try to hold back. I didn't know where to focus, pinned between them like this. Every touch was simple on its own, but incredible when put together.

As I lost myself in mounting pleasure, my touch fell away from Colin. He pressed closer, grinding against my exposed hip, his erection and zipper digging into my skin with a delicious burn.

My breath came in short gasps. Colin crushed his mouth to mine, swallowing my cries as I came hard, using Tanner's hand to stroke until the touch was too much and I had to force him away.

"Holy fuck, that was way better than doing that myself." Did I say that out loud?

Colin's short laugh confirmed I had. "I'd hope so." His grin was sheepish and smug at the same time. Irresistibly-sexy-meets-boy-next-door.

Tanner pulled his hand away gently, and I couldn't help but follow as he raised his fingers to his mouth and sucked one clean. "Your pussy tastes so good." The guttural words yanked me back into the moment.

Colin stepped past me to glide his tongue up Tanner's fingers, then press his lips in for a kiss. Seeing their kiss was as scorching as watching them share my taste, especially when Tanner gripped the back of Colin's neck and held him tight. Their groans lit my body on fire.

I'd almost be content to sit back and watch the two of them consume each other, but I'd been promised a threesome, and I wanted to see what came next.

When Tanner and Colin broke apart, I swore the air between them was going to combust. Colin turned away first, like he had downstairs, and Tanner shifted his attention to me. There was no stretching or craning my neck to make this kiss work. Tanner dove in with concentrated intensity as he shoved my top to the floor then stripped off his own shirt.

His skin was hot against mine, his kisses demanding and desperate. With his hands on my hips, he moved backwards toward the bed, until he was sitting on the mattress. He drew me into his lap.

I straddled his legs and draped my arms around his neck. "All these layers of clothing between us will lead to a lot of dry humping." I had to tease him or I'd lose myself in his ferocity.

"It'll also keep me from coming too fast." His voice was an octave lower than normal.

I was tempted to push him back and grind against him, see if I could make the coming happen regard-less. I was also intently aware Colin was still here and I wanted them both. Besides, Colin had to be a safer option for keeping my wits. "I have an easier solution."

"Oh?" Tanner cocked an eyebrow.

When I stood, his grunt of disappointment was

tangible. I turned to Colin and brushed my lips over his. He knotted his fingers in my hair and crushed our mouths together.

I was so wrong—this wasn't safety, it was purity combined with intoxication.

In a frantic tumble of limbs and attempting to feel everything about each other, we managed to get each other's clothes off. His cock sprang up the instant it was released—no wonder he didn't need a fancy car. No need to compensate here.

I wrapped my fingers around the shaft, stroking slowly as Colin pulled me in for more kisses. "You have condoms?" I didn't know who I was asking. I had some in my purse, and would go get them if I had to, but I'd rather not take a break from this incredible moment.

Colin nodded.

Tanner kissed along my bare shoulder. The way his dick left an impression on my ass, he'd lost the rest of his clothes, too. "I want to watch you ride him," he said.

Colin chuckled. "I thought you were the one who liked being the main event."

"The two of you are the exception." Tanner's words caressed my soul. "Alone. Together. Whatever." He slid a condom between us.

I grabbed the foil package, and used my full body to nudge Colin toward the bed. Flavored condom? Had to be Tanner's, but I had no complaints. As Colin laid down I tore the rubber free. He was too thick to do my favorite trick well, but I could improvise. I rolled the condom down a few inches with my mouth, finishing the job with my fingers.

The twin groans of appreciation that I received for the brief show were fuel on the fire raging inside me. I kept my lips wrapped around Colin, my hand at the base of his shaft, and sucked hungrily on his cock.

"So good." He grabbed my arms and I lifted my head. "But you're gonna make me come, and I'm not ready for that yet."

Two guys, at once, who both cared about lasting long enough to draw out the fun. Could I ever go back to normal sex again?

I slid up Colin's body, intently aware of Tanner's scorching gaze on us. I brushed my breasts over Colin's cock, then my stomach, finally straddling his legs and hovering over his erection.

He grabbed his shaft, slid to nudge my opening, and thrust his hips up. The way he stretched me out put my favorite dildo to shame. And then he was gripping my hips hard. Hammering inside me. Pressing his thumb to my clit, which was both too sensitive and not enough so, and my body didn't know how to react.

Tanner pressed into me from behind, bringing the frantic fucking to a pause. He kissed along my shoulder and nipped at my earlobe. "Do you think you can take us both at once? He glided a lubed-up finger to nudge tease my rear entrance.

"God, I want to try." I didn't mean to say that aloud, but I was glad I had.

Tanner urged me to lean forward until my chest was pressed to Colin's. He reached behind me to spread my ass cheeks, and Tanner slipped the head of his dick along the same path his finger had traveled a moment ago.

I'd had anal sex before—with other men, with my toys... I had to be incredibly turned on and in a mood to want it, and right now I was both. I relaxed as Tanner pushed in, and was grateful he knew better than to rush.

His slow penetration gave me time to appreciate how different this new sensation was. Both of them in me, the wall between their cocks thin, and the friction high. *Wow.*

They started rocking again, a slow build to a steady speed. Colin pushed me up and lowered his head enough to draw one of my nipples into his mouth, while Tanner reached between us and settled his finger on my clit. There was so much stimulation that it flew past uncomfortable and toward incredible.

"I want to hear what you sound like when you scream with pleasure." Tanner drew his fingers over my swollen bud the same way I'd done with him earlier. "I need to hear that gorgeous voice. Come for me again?"

I swore his permission was all I needed. Orgasm washed over me, stealing my breath and thoughts and forcing a scream of pleasure from my lungs. As the feeling ebbed, another crashed around me. I lost myself in bliss, and rode the high, only vaguely aware that the guys' hands had fallen away.

Tanner's grunts grew louder and more punctuated until they drew into a long groan, and slowed to a stop. He kept rocking with us, though he wasn't sliding in and out of me anymore.

Colin's face screwed up, like a stunning, orgasmic angel, a shudder rocked through his body, and he came as well.

I fell onto his chest, and Tanner rested his weight against my back, as we all struggled to catch our breath. I may never get the chance to do this again, and I was burning this amazing moment into my mind forever.

THE SUN WAS UP, streaming through my blinds, and I was still in bed. Sure, it was barely seven, but I couldn't remember the last time I slept this late and wasn't filled with panic at the realization. I didn't have work today. Or kids. Or… anything but two gorgeous younger men pressing against me as we floated toward consciousness.

Colin's groan amplified my reluctance to move. "I need to get ready. I don't want to move, though."

"Me neither." I liked waking up to this view. His bright eyes watching me through dark lashes, and a tiny smile on his face.

"Five more minutes?" Tanner pressed into my back, his skin hot and tempting against mine.

I'd stay here all day if I thought it was an option.

Colin pushed into a sitting position, cracking the serene bubble around us. He scrubbed his face. "So how does this work now?"

How accustomed was he to one-night stands?

"We go back to life." Tanner's reply didn't carry his typical confidence.

The situation was what it was. "There's no commitment here. I won't say last night was *just* sex —it was incredible sex"—so incredible—"but this isn't a matter of *we did it and now we have to get married*."

One corner of Colin's mouth tugged up. "But it's okay that I liked it."

"It'd be way less okay if you didn't," Tanner said.

"But it shouldn't happen again?" Colin was definitely giving off a *this is all new to me* vibe.

And I was okay with the questions. Each one made sense and made me wish I'd had a chance to ask the same thing the first time I went home with a random guy. I'd made so many assumptions since then, and Colin was letting me admit to myself this wasn't something people just knew how to do.

"I wouldn't put pressure on future hookups, one way or another," I said. In my head, that wasn't the answer most guys wanted to hear, but I would've liked to, and I suspected Colin would too. Besides, I wanted the two of them to have another chance or two together… and I was having a hard time accepting I might not be involved.

"So, really, no pressure from either direction," Colin said.

"Never."

I was surprised with how quickly Tanner's reply came.

Colin's expression was hard to read. "I should get to work. Thank you for last night. For all of it."

As he climbed out of bed, I couldn't take my gaze off his bare ass. When he pulled up his boxers, I forced myself to look away. A glance at Tanner showed a similar reaction. Was he staring too or did I just want him to be? For Colin's sake.

Colin gave one more tiny wave, and then I heard his footsteps fading as he walked down the stairs.

"In answer to your question." Tanner's statement caught me off-guard.

I turned to him. "Which one?" Had I asked a question?

"Yesterday evening, you asked why I was hitting on you."

Not quite my words, but I supposed my meaning. "Right." It seemed like so long ago.

"When I say this, it's not a line. Do you believe me?"

"Hard to know without hearing what you have to say." This was a bit surreal, sitting naked in bed with this gorgeous, cocky man, and having what felt like an adult conversation.

Tanner sighed. "That's fair. Instead then, will you trust me when I tell you that I mean it."

He was building this up a bit, whatever it was, and I had a hard time with certain kinds of trust. My agreement sounded important to him, though, and I believed the things Tanner said, even when I thought they were arrogant, over the top, or cheesy. "I trust you."

"You're attractive, you're fun to be around, and I enjoy your company. Last night seemed like a good opportunity to explore desire further. But then you..." He raked his fingers through his hair.

"Not used to hearing *no*?"

He winced. "I'm not used to a woman—any person—who knows what they want out of life the way you do."

The unexpected compliment warmed me and made me laugh at the same time. "I'm not that put together, I just put on a good show."

"An amazing one." He leaned in and pressed his lips to my cheek. "It's super hot. I'm going to the pool to do laps. Thank you for last night."

And then Tanner was gone too.

I had no idea what to do with myself, especially with so many thoughts bouncing in my head about last night and this morning.

11
daria

My bed was empty except for me. Not unusual, but it left me feeling more alone than normal. As I rolled my head to the side, a bottle of lube—the tiny one I usually kept in the bathroom cabinet—made me smile at the memories of last night. Now I knew where Tanner got that. I was a bit relieved he hadn't had KY in his pocket.

My schedule was as empty as my bed. Very unusual. I had a text from Kandace telling me she'd better not catch any hint I was working today. What was I supposed to do?

Alana loved to tell me about all the things she was going to do when she was an adult that were things I didn't allow. She'd be pretty bummed to know one thing I couldn't do was call my friends in the middle of the day and say *let's hang out*. Carly was in Italy. Actually, she was probably somewhere over the

Midwest right about now, since her plane got in this afternoon.

That meant she'd be taking the rest of the week off. I could snag some of her time tomorrow, but when she landed today she'd want to sleep off the jet lag and time zone change. I'd known Carly forever, and she worked for the same angel investment firm I did. No one was better at appraising a property being considered as part of an investment. She could find the flaws a buyer didn't want someone to see, or uncover things that weren't nearly as bad as the lending bank tried to claim, and our firm flew her all over the world to make sure their money was going into the right properties.

I sent her a quick text telling her we should have coffee tomorrow, then called Dustin. I'd passed that point in my life where it was embarrassing to say my brother was one of my best friends, and I liked his partners, too.

"Yellow," Dustin answered cheerfully.

I could make small talk, but that wasn't us. "Where are you going for lunch?"

"Are you looking for suggestions? When you're in Hawaii you don't have McDonalds. Go find some local hole in the wall."

I snorted a laugh. "Like you *ever* eat at McDonalds. And I'm not in Hawaii." The second bit of my reply came out softly.

"What happened?"

"Work. And since the Disneyland thing with Joe… But now work is done."

"I get it."

I knew he would. A decade ago, Dustin would've given me grief over sacrificing a vacation because work asked, but my circumstances were extreme and his work habits were a lot less healthy than mine now.

"Speaking of…" He trailed off.

"You're on a tight deadline and working through lunch?" And probably dinner.

"Bingo."

I smiled at the empty room. "I get it."

Dustin laughed. "Go take a drive. Head into the canyons and have lunch. Something. Enjoy the time to yourself."

"Maybe." The idea sounded fun, but I felt so strange not doing… anything. Come to think of it, I may have struggled to unwind going on vacation by myself anyway. I'd ask Dustin if he wanted to have dinner at any point this week, but he wouldn't be free and neither would his partners, since they all worked together. "Tell Adrienne and Phillip I said *hi*."

"I will. Don't work."

I rolled my eyes. "Byeee."

I flopped back on my bed. Now what?

Fuck it. I needed to be busy and now seemed like the perfect time to do those little things around the house that were always waiting until I had more time. I made three lists on my phone, one for today, tomorrow, and Friday. I'd start small with replacing the interior doorknobs on the main floor to match the rest of the house, and deodorizing the carpet to get rid of the lingering cheese puff dust I was pretty sure was causing a faint funky smell.

When I stepped into the shower, a large dildo suction cupped to the seat winked back at me. Did Tanner see that? He'd have to be blind not to. At least it didn't seem to change his impression of me, or maybe it had a little to do with why he came on so strong last night.

I wanted to be mortified, but I'd had his cock inside me, so we were probably past the point of this being TMI. And speaking of… Memories of last night would make any morning masturbation routine pale in comparison, so the dildo was going back in its drawer.

Shower done, hair pulled back, and toy stashed, I was on my way to the hardware store. I never knew where to find the little things here—the way this place was organized didn't make sense to me. But an hour later, I had what I needed and I was home again.

I finished the doorknob on the half-bath off the kitchen, and was working on the one for the room Colin was staying in when I had the weirdest sensation I was being watched. I looked up and found Colin standing next to me, and my heart tried to leap from my chest. "Holy shit, you scared me."

"Sorry." He chuckled. "You didn't hear me come in."

"I didn't expect anyone home for a while."

He shrugged. "Deacon—the guy whose place I'm doing the painting in—had to close early for a family emergency. Are you evicting us and changing the locks already?" His teasing was undercut with the faintest hint of concern.

"I mean, once you give a guy a key to your place, he thinks he lives there or something," I teased.

Colin's smile was the kind of sweetness and sincerity that could melt a person's insides. "The nerve of some men. Do you need any help?"

"This would be easier with a second set of hands."

"I'll put my hands wherever you tell me to." Colin winced. "That came out wrong, didn't it?"

So different from Tanner, and adorably sexy in his own way. "I think it sounded exactly the way you wanted it to," I said.

"If you call me on shit like that, I'll have to clean up my act."

"Never change for someone else." I paused and replayed my response in my head. "That came out way more seriously than I meant it to."

Colin smirked. "Where do you want me boss?"

Face buried between my legs, using that skilled tongue of his.

Just because we didn't put limits on future encounters, didn't mean I needed to be daydreaming about jumping their bones every chance I got. "Hand me the next screw then hold this exactly where it is." I nodded at the doorknob.

"Just assume there are going to be a lot of *screw* jokes racing through my head as we do this." He handed me the hardware.

"Assume it's the same for me."

The work went a lot faster with Colin's help, and I was double grateful he was there when it came time to push the couches to the edge of the living room.

"Explain this cheese puffs thing to me again," Colin said. "I'm missing something. There's not a speck of visible dirt in your house, but you're worried about cheese in the carpet?"

Because I'd cleaned the place top to bottom before they arrived, and I had someone come in three times a week to stay on top of the mess. I tugged on my ponytail. "We bought this powder, and Harmony used way too much on the popcorn, then spilled the bowl on the floor in front of the TV. I've vacuumed a couple of times, but I can smell it still. That faint, decaying fake cheese scent."

Colin wrinkled his nose. "You make it sound so appetizing."

"It's a gift." I grabbed the deodorizer I'd bought at the hardware store, and sprinkled it liberally on the carpet. "The instructions say I have to wait before I vacuum it up. Wanna split that last beer with me?"

"Ms. Lane, are you trying to get me drunk to take advantage of me?" Colin's scandalized voice rose an octave.

"Not at all. I want you completely sober when I take advantage of you." Was that kind of joking allowed, especially with Colin? I had no idea. "But seriously, I just want to get it out of the fridge."

Colin bowed and gestured toward the kitchen. "Sounds reasonable. After you."

I grabbed the last beer from the fridge and turned to find Colin already waiting with the bottle opener. He popped the top. I took a short swallow and handed the drink to him.

"Tanner's missing all the fun," I teased.

A shadow crossed over Colin's face, but it vanished so quickly I could have imagined it. "You can recruit him to help tomorrow," Colin said.

Weird. "I don't have anything nearly as interesting as installing doorknobs planned. I'm cleaning grout."

"Maybe you could get him to put on a maid outfit and help."

"A boy maid or a girl maid?" Because I could picture Tanner in a short black skirt that did nothing to hide those iron swimmer's thighs. An unpleasant whiff of something reached me and I wrinkled my nose. That wasn't me, was it? "Do you smell that?" I was almost afraid to ask.

Colin wore a similar expression. He lifted his arms and sniffed. "Pretty sure it's not me."

The smell was stronger now, and giving me flash-backs to my sorority days before I learned not to mix hard liquors. I followed my nose toward the living room, the scent growing more potent and vile with each step. Was it starting to burn my eyes?

12

tanner

I LEARNED a long time ago how to turn off my brain while I was swimming or otherwise working out, so it was an easy decision for me to head straight for the pool after I left Daria's. If I stopped to think, I'd dwell on last night. I couldn't do that.

With my camera set up in its normal place, I dove into my personal time trials. I pushed until my body ached and my muscles screamed. I was so close to hitting my mark. Less than a second away. But my body wasn't having it anymore; I needed to call it a morning.

I spent the next hour stretching, making sure I was careful with my shoulder, and doing all the exercises that became second-nature after physical therapy.

The instant I stopped, stripped, and stepped into the shower, my mind turned on again.

Last night was incredible—holy fuck, Daria blew

my fantasies about her out of the water. She was an amazing combination of reserved and bold that made me want to unwrap her and explore her for hours. Again and again. Her body. Her mind.

I expected I'd discover something new every time.

I was glad no one else was in the locker room, to see my dick standing at attention in agreement. I dried off and dressed, clinging desperately to thoughts of Daria.

As I headed out to the parking lot, I lost my grip on the images of her, and Colin slammed in to take her place. I swore I could still feel his lips crushed to mine. The scruff of stubble burning my skin. The hunger in that connection. Enough that I'd been tempted to ask him for more than a kiss.

As I was walking out, John was coming in.

"Hold up." I stopped him. "Do you have a minute?"

"Sure."

"The building, are you selling it because of maintenance problems?" I wasn't in the mood for subtext. Might as well ask him outright.

He stared back, shock on his face. "It does need work, yes. The other half hasn't been open in a while and smells like chlorine. The HVAC over there needs work. But there's nothing structurally wrong with it. No cracks in the foundation or anything like that."

He sounded sincere, and usually I could read those things. Though, if I'd misread my feelings for Colin all these years—

Whoa, where did that come from?

"Cool. The bank was asking me some questions, so I'll pass that along. Catch you around." Either John was full of shit or Davenport had heard wrong. The second option seemed more likely, but John wasn't going to tell me *yeah, the place is falling apart* if he wanted to sell.

I didn't know what to think. About anything.

The library beckoned—a quiet place with no reminders or chances of running into my distractions.

Colin came out as bisexual when as we started high school. I hadn't seen it coming; sometimes the obvious escaped me. I spent a lot of time wondering if maybe I was the same, bisexual or gay, and hadn't realized that either. The pondering involved trying to imagine myself kissing other men. Kissing Colin. Asking Colin to help me experiment and figure it out.

One thing hadn't escaped me though—Colin put up with a lot of teasing when he came out. I'd done everything I could to shut it down, and I never wanted him to think I was adding to it by saying *hey, make out with me to see if I like it*.

Beyond that, I couldn't picture myself with another guy, and I *really* liked girls.

The easy answer was that I must be straight.

When I got settled into an isolated room in the library, I expected to lose myself in work, the way I had in my workout. I was looking up bankers and other contacts for loans, emailing, and hustling like crazy.

Sure I noticed when a man was attractive, but I couldn't imagine myself *with* them. Going back to Daria's questions last night, even when I was fucking around, hooking up with the male athletes didn't appeal to me.

It had a little bit to do with the fact that homosexuality wasn't only barely becoming acceptable in athletic forums. An athlete never knew who might out them. But I hadn't missed the experience, or been disappointed that I couldn't have it.

But after last night...

Was the experience stuck in my head because it was new and amazing, or because I wanted more? From Colin? From someone else?

I tried for a few hours to get through my work. This would be so much easier if I knew anyone who worked with this kind of loan. True, contacts weren't always necessary, but we were looking for a significant amount of money, and being able to drop a name or two would make a difference.

With a dozen emails sent off, and thoughts of last night still racing through my mind, I packed up my stuff to head back to the pool for another practice run.

There were two texts from Colin as I left the library.

Where are you?

When you get to Daria's, we're upstairs. I'll explain then.

Jealousy surged inside, so intense I felt it in my neck. Who did I envy more—Colin or Daria? This kind of reaction didn't belong in one-night stands, but telling myself that didn't push the feeling aside.

Thoughts of the pool were gone, I needed to be at Daria's instead, whether or not it was a rational decision. When I stepped inside her place, the smell hit me hard. It was vomit carried on heavy, warm air. The back doors and windows were open, and two box fans sat near the patio door, blowing out.

Was someone sick? Concern filtered through me.

I headed upstairs. Daria's door was closed, and her laughter mingled with Colin's and flitted into the hallway. Worry plus envy meant I was the one who was going to be ill. I knocked.

"S'open," Daria called.

I pushed into the room.

"But close it fast," she added quickly. She was sitting on her bed in a lightweight tank top and thin shorts, and it was obvious she wasn't wearing a bra. The distinct topography of her chest--aka her rock-hard nipples—also accentuated the fact that it was about ten degrees cooler in here than in the rest of the house.

Colin sat next to her, not wearing much more, and they were both flushed and smiling.

I wasn't used to being at a loss for words. "What happened?" It wasn't a complicated question, but it covered a lot of territory.

Daria laughed and ducked her head. "Impromptu chemistry lesson."

The kind that showed what kind of sparks I swore

were flying between the two of them? I had no right, but that didn't stop me from stewing in jealousy.

13
colin

"WHAT KIND OF CHEMISTRY?" Tanner asked. There was no way he was watching us with jealousy. I'd been trying to get him to notice me for how long, and he was hooked on Daria in a night? After all that bullshit about casual hookups?

I wasn't quite being fair, since we'd known Daria for longer than a day or two, and I could absolutely see myself spending more time with her. Not just because of last night, but after today, too.

And wow I was bad at getting over Tanner. I wanted them both again. And again. "We learned if you mix the wrong kind of carpet powder with powdered cheese"—I wrinkled my nose—"*whew* it's bad. You smelled it when you got here, but it was *way* worse a few hours ago."

"Air's off to keep the smell from circulating, the windows are open downstairs to get rid of the stench, and someone is coming tomorrow to fix my mistake,"

Daria said. "Until then, we're self-quarantined in our own little biome for the night."

Tanner's entire posture changed as he relaxed.

Daria patted the mattress. "Kick off your shoes and join us. Tell us about your day."

He didn't hesitate, and I was surprised he sat next to me rather than diving between Daria and me. There was enough distance between us that I couldn't feel him, but he was still close enough to reach out and grab my neck and pull me in for a kiss. A long, heavy, hungry—

"Well?" I asked partly to keep my mind from wandering and at least a little because Tanner was quiet.

"Well what?"

This was odd for him, not launching into conversation any chance he got. "How was your day?" I poked his arm. "Are you sure you're Tanner?" He felt like Tanner. *Fuck*, I could dig my fingers into those biceps and just hold on for dear life.

Any resolve I had from yesterday was already shot. One taste, and I wanted him more than ever. The way I'd been sitting up here with Daria laughing over the simplest things, like the most ridiculous versus the best swimsuit episodes in anime, made me want her more too. Knowing both desires were doomed didn't dampen either one.

"It was a fantastic day." Tanner's trademark grin was back, brighter than I expected.

Too bright? Nah. "Just like that? No details?"

"I'm milliseconds from making my qualifying time," Tanner said.

"That is fantastic. Way to go." I offered him a high five. One more chance at the Olympics meant more to him than anything, and I wanted him to have that.

Daria gave him a quick hug. "That's awesome, seriously."

Why couldn't I be that casual? Because we were guys and I'd take my own gestures wrong. *Sigh.*

"But it wasn't all good." I couldn't ignore that something was off.

Tanner shrugged. "It's harder than I thought finding people at banks to talk to me, and I'm getting conflicting information about the condition of the building." He looked at me. "I need your time and talent, to make this proposal shine."

"You've got it. I'll be done with the mural in a few days, and you can have me any other time we're not in lessons." I winced mentally at my own phrasing. "Daria knows people, and she's offered to help us…"

"And I mean it. In fact, Carly will take a look at the building for you and tell you exactly what's up," Daria said. "I'll ask her tomorrow. And I'm happy to give your proposal a look and give you some lender names. I'd hook you up at work, but you don't want investors. Not until you decide to franchise. You want a loan that you pay off and you're done."

"What's a Carly?" I asked.

"My best friend, my sanity, and the best fucking commercial appraiser in the world."

Tanner wrinkled his nose. "We can't."

"Can't what? Why not?" I'd missed something.

"We can't ask Daria for help. This is her job."

Daria raised her brows. "You teach my girls to swim."

"You pay us for it," Tanner said.

Daria sighed. "We're friends. Aren't we? Friends help friends, and I know what I'm offering."

The more time I spent with her, the more I found about her to adore. Was I doomed to crush on everyone who was nice to me? I wasn't having these hang-ups with Deacon. Was it because I knew he'd reciprocate? "We'd love your help."

Tanner glared at me.

"If it makes you feel better, we'll give Alana six months of lessons free," I added.

Daria pursed her lips. "It doesn't make *me* feel better. This is important to you and I can help. You'll hurt my feelings if you tell me *no*."

Tanner's smile wasn't as potent this time, but it looked more genuine. "All right. Thank you."

She clapped once. "Good. Now that we have that settled, what's on the agenda for tonight?"

"Do we need an agenda?" I wasn't great with plans. I didn't mind them, and I was fine with sticking to other people's timelines and schedules, but left on my own? I did whatever struck my fancy.

Daria shrugged. "I made a to-do list earlier just to have a schedule. I'm not quite sure what to do with myself without tasks waiting." She seemed to need this.

"What would you like to put on the agenda?" My asking was much better than my assuming.

"I don't know."

"If I might make a suggestion," Tanner said.

I gestured to him. "I'll open the floor. Tanner, what should we put on the agenda?"

"Karaoke."

That was always fun. I loved karaoke.

The way Daria wrinkled her nose wasn't encouraging. "I don't know."

"If this is about you not liking your singing voice or something, I know you can carry a tune, I heard you humming earlier. And it's not like we're musical masters." Though we weren't bad. Tanner and I were my favorite road trip car duo.

"I'm not worried about that," Daria said. "I did competition choir in high school and college. I *am* worried about making the two of you look bad." She winked.

"As if." I stared back in disbelief.

Tanner laughed. "That sounds like a challenge."

"This isn't a competition," I reminded him.

"*Everything* is a competition." Tanner's voice was light, but the words left an uncomfortable pebble in my gut.

"*Besides,*" Daria's voice kept my brain from running away with the thought. "You're not going to like any of my old lady music."

I snorted a laugh. "You're anything but an old lady."

"You realize there's only eight years between us," Tanner added.

Daria twisted her mouth. "There are almost eight years between Alana and Harmony, and that's a lifetime."

"Yes. In fact, it's more than Harmony's lifetime." I wasn't big on debate or arguing, but she was wrong about this. "This is different."

The way Daria looked at me, she wasn't convinced. "Eight years is almost a third of your lifetime."

"Whatever you're trying to prove, it's not working," Tanner said. "Pick a song and we'll match you word for word."

I heard the challenge in Tanner's voice—he really was turning this into a competition. Though if the prize was to convince Daria she wasn't old and we weren't kids, I was in. "*When I Grow Up* by Garbage." I picked before she could come back with another disagreement.

"You're going to sing that." Daria radiated disbelief.

I nodded.

"Do you need lyrics?"

"Nope." I extracted myself from the bed, reluctantly leaving the comfort of being between Daria and Tanner behind.

"Xerxes, play *When I Grow Up*, by Garbage," Daria

said to the home smart system. "Music only, no vocal tracks."

Now I was feeling that spirit of competition.

Tanner whistled and clapped as the song started up.

I didn't miss a beat, sliding into "Bah bah bah bah, bah bah bah bah," as the first changeover happened. Years ago, I struggled with this—even singing for a single other person—but Tanner had been amazingly patient helping me get past the fear.

Now it was easy to headbang when the beat required it, and let myself move as I sang the familiar song. The frequent claps and whistles from both Tanners and Daria made it even better tonight.

When the song finished, I took a bow, to a standing applause. Ridiculous, but also fun.

"Incredible." Daria's skepticism seemed to have vanished.

"But that song? Quietly fucked up," Tanner said.

I liked it regardless. "You've got better?"

"Xerxes, play *Simply Irresistible*."

Daria laughed. "Xerxes, do not do that. Cancel."

"Do you have a problem with that song?" Tanner asked.

Daria shook her head. "But it's not the same without the women in black dresses and red lipstick."

"Tell me you don't own both. We'll wait right here if you want to change." Tanner rested his arms behind him, leaned his weight back, and stretched his legs out on the mattress.

Daria laughed harder. "I do not. Xerxes, play *Don't You Want Me* by The Human League."

"I don't know that one." Tanner pouted.

How did he manage to make that look sexy instead of childish? "I do." I grasped Daria's hand and tugged her to her feet.

The angsty duet kicked off, and I sang my part without missing a beat. When the first female section kicked in, Daria held my gaze while she sang in the most incredible voice. I was stunned enough I almost missed my cue when it was my turn again.

Somehow we managed to move closer with each exchange, but never actually touched each other. As the music finished, I couldn't look away from her flushed face and the short heaves of her chest.

Tanner's applause broke the mood. "Absolutely amazing. However, you're both depressing, even if you hide it under a pair of great voices, and you don't get to pick the next song. Xerxes, play *The Look*."

He moved to the other side of Daria, spun her to face him, and started singing along with the music. A tiny smile played on her face, and I had to move to get a better view.

When Tanner sang about a brown-eyed girl being blue, he tilted Daria's chin up, and her lips parted in a silent gasp. When a chorus of *na na na na nas* kicked in, the two of them went back and forth, shimmying and grinding and harmonizing. I expected a surge of jealousy, but heat flooded me instead. I *liked* watching them together.

We worked our way through several more songs, the sexual tension in the room growing with each one. It didn't matter what someone picked, there was a reason to grind against someone else.

I was riding the high of impulsiveness and fun when Tanner finished *Opportunities* by The Pet Shop Boys. I nudged Tanner and Daria to sit on the edge of the bed. "Your phone controls the music too?"

Daria lay back to grab it off her night stand, treating me to an incredible view of her stretched out, then sat up again and handed it to me. "It does. Is your next song a surprise?"

"It is." I pulled up the music, and handed the device back.

Twin expressions of surprise met me when George Michael's *Father Figure* started. My reservations were gone as I lost myself in the song, moving to kneel in front of Tanner, hold his gaze, and let the lyrics and soulful tune wrap me up in a world separate from reality.

I rose halfway, hands on Tanner's knees, never looking away from him, as I sang the final line about being the one who would love him until the end of time.

When the music stopped, I was nose to nose with Tanner, who stared back with wide eyes. A couple of inches closer and I'd kiss him. If I did that, I wouldn't have the strength to pull away tonight, but if I initiated and *he* pulled away, I didn't know what I'd do.

14

tanner

It was just a song.

Colin picked it because he liked it.

He focused on me because it would be weird to sing things like *love you until the end of time* to Daria. And of course we loved each other. Best friends. Bros forever.

It didn't matter that him being so close was making my pulse race. That the faint scent of paint thinner mingled with aftershave in a way that was distinctly Colin and clogging my sinuses. And it didn't matter that his deep, soulful voice, and the way he hadn't looked away when the music stopped had my dick rock hard.

It was just a song.

Fuck it.

I grabbed his face, and crushed my mouth to his. I didn't know where his groan stopped and mine started. His stubble was rough against my mouth, his fingers dug into my thighs, and fuck if I didn't want this to go on and on.

A soft gasp next to me drilled into my thoughts enough to remind me we weren't alone, but it didn't shatter the need thrumming under my skin. I broke the kiss with a grunt and forced my gaze to Daria.

Who was here because this was her bedroom and her house and how did that slip my mind for even a second?

"I can leave if you want." Her tone was playful and she jerked a thumb toward the door.

"No." Colin cleared his throat and stood. "Don't be ridiculous." His voice was still gravel.

Mine would probably be as bad. This was where I should say *it was just a kiss* or *it wasn't a big deal.* "What's next on the agenda?" I managed to sound normal, but I certainly didn't feel it. What was going on with my body? My head?

"Hang on. We're not done with the previous conversation." Colin was back to himself as well. "I want to know, Daria, if we hadn't stopped, what were you going to do?"

I wanted to know that too.

Pink spread across her cheeks. "Hope you didn't mind me watching."

And now I was even harder. How was that possible? I also refused to lose control of this situation. "You like watching, then?"

"It all depends on the who and the what. I like it best when I can tell everyone's enjoying themselves."

She managed both demure and confident in a single response.

Colin dropped onto the mattress next to me, his thigh brushing mine and sending another wash of desire through me.

"I'm all about everyone enjoying themselves," I said.

Daria's playful smile threatened to undo me. "So you've said."

I rested a hand on Colin's thigh, high enough to feel his heat without me making contact. I looked him in the eye. "What do you think? Interested in enjoying ourselves a bit more?"

"I don't know." The way Colin licked his lips then caught the bottom one between his teeth was as enticing as Daria's smile. "Sure."

His agreement was all I needed. I gripped the back of his neck and kissed him again, devouring his groans, biting his lips and memorizing every sound and feeling. I used my body to push him further up on the bed, straddled his legs, and pinned his arms above his head.

With my weight pressed into him, I felt every bit of his hard body, including his erection digging into my stomach. Through his thin shorts and my T-shirt, the thrust of his hips was obvious.

Fuck, I wanted more. I cupped his cock and stroked in time with his grind.

Colin gripped my wrist. "Stop."

His strained request took a heartbeat to sink in,

and I paused. I raised myself on my wrists enough to look him in the eye.

"Don't do this to turn someone else on. Not even her."

"I'm not—"

Colin moved his palm to my chest and pushed me away, holding me at arm's length. "Think carefully about what you say and do next. Hard and horny is not the best time to make a decision like the one you're about to make."

"Are you telling me you don't want to do this?" Obviously. Duh, me.

"Not tonight. Not like this."

I forced myself to pull away completely. I raked my fingers through my hair as I sat up. Stopping physically didn't stop the arousal, take away my hardon, or obliterate the thoughts about kisses and cocks and Daria watching us.

But the few inches of space gave me enough air to breathe and reality sank in. What had I almost done to my friendship with Colin? Please don't let it be irreversible.

I scrubbed my face, put some more distance between all three of us, and adjusted myself as best I could. "Okay, then. Now what?"

As I glanced at Colin then Daria, neither looked back.

This was exactly what I didn't want, but I'd caused it in my desperate need to get laid. Time to fix it. I clapped once. "Like Colin said, let's not do things this way tonight."

"Not what I meant," Colin muttered.

But it wasn't in opposition of what he meant, either. "Hands up if you regret last night," I said.

Neither of them moved.

"So, we all have wonderful memories. We're all cool, like we said this morning? It was mind blowing sex and none of us wants to take it back?"

Colin shrugged, but it looked like he was fighting a smile.

One corner of Daria's mouth tugged up and she met my gaze. "Do we have to raise our hands to ask a question, too?"

"You didn't raise your hand, so obviously not," I teased.

Her smile grew. "I didn't want anyone to think I had regrets."

"We should do something not-sexy," Colin said.

I understood his point, but I wished I didn't. "Three people with incredible chemistry sharing a bed? It's all sexy."

Daria snorted. "That's such a man thing to say."

"You disagree?" I kept my tone light, but I didn't try to hide the challenge in my question.

"No, but I know better than to say it out loud."

"We could watch movies." Colin still sounded flat. He wasn't quite with us.

There had to be some way to help him feel more at ease again.

"What's the least sexy movie you can think of?" Daria asked.

My balls ached and my brain was still trying to work on a less than optimal blood supply, but I was an adult and I could think through arousal without getting off. And maybe make Colin smile again. *"Fantastic Four."*

"The ones with Chris Evans or the remake?" Colin went straight for the bait.

Daria's mouth formed an *O*. "He's pretty sexy."

Colin felt the same and he never made a secret of it. "She said *least sexy* movie, not *worst* movie." Some of the playfulness was emerging in Colin's voice.

I scoffed. "Worst movie I can think of is *Justice League*."

"How dare you?" Daria's shrill disdain was exaggerated.

Colin grinned. "Aquaman gives him performance anxiety."

I couldn't believe he went there. I grabbed a pillow and lobbed it at him.

Daria snagged it out of the air with a smoothness that most basketball coaches wished could be taught. "Pillow fights are definitely sexy."

"In movies. They're not in real life," Colin said with a kind of authority that implied he had personal experience.

Did he? Because now I was picturing Daria and Colin, in their lightweight clothing with minimal to no support, bouncing around on the bed, trying to avoid pillows. That would definitely be sexy. I knew better than to say it aloud this time. "*Game of Thrones.*"

Colin's expression faltered. "There are tits and peens everywhere."

"But would you call it sexy?" Apparently a lot of things turned me on, but Hodor's dick never had.

Daria shook her head. "I would not. Let's do it." She grabbed a remote from the bedside table and turned on the TV over her dresser.

We settled in to watch the show, each of us picking a different spot on the bed to sit. It was disappointing but it made sense. Colin and I had seen the first few seasons multiple times, and it was clear from the way Daria bounced her commentary off ours that she had too.

About the time Ned Stark arrived in King's Landing, Daria's phone rang. She glanced at the screen. "My own small council beckons. Be right back." She stepped out of the room and was closing the door before she said "Hey, Sweetie. How was your day?"

Her kids.

Silence settled between Colin and I with Daria gone. The TV provided the dialog, but the Mystery Science Theater Three Thousand commentary vanished.

I didn't want to feel uncomfortable around Colin. "Are we good?" I made sure to push the sincerity into my question.

"We're good." Colin nodded. He sounded like he meant it. "You can sit up here if you promise to keep your hands to yourself." Was he joking as he patted the spot next to him?

Thank fuck. "Cross my heart." I moved to sit with my back to the headboard, still keeping distance between us, but not nearly as much as before. This was better.

Daria came back a short while later. "Alana says *hi*" she relayed as she joined us on the bed.

The reminder of our actual relationship with Daria, and that next week we'd go back to our lives and this would become just a pleasant memory, pretty much killed the last of my sexy thoughts.

We went back to the show and our play by play, but as each new episode rolled, we said less and yawned more.

I didn't remember falling asleep, but the sun outside the window said it was morning. Daria was breathing steadily, her back to me and her ass pressed into me. And fuck if I wasn't hard again.

I should extract myself from this situation before she woke up.

She wiggled against me. "Is that your sword, Jon Snow?"

"Are you talking to me or him?" Sleep lined Colin's question.

So much for leaving. Not that I really wanted to.

"Both of you, apparently." Daria giggled.

That was adorable. I rested a hand on her hip. I was glad Colin stopped me last night, but this wasn't me pushing for sex with another man to get someone else off.

"Are you offering to help me sheath my blade?" It was tempting to slip my fingers under the elastic of her shorts, and tease her bare skin, but I could take things a *little* slowly.

Daria glanced over her shoulder at me, a teasing smile on her face. "I'm offering to watch you do it yourself."

"Did you just tell him to go fuck himself?" Colin asked.

Daria laughed. "No, though I can see now why you'd think that." She extracted herself from between us and crawled away, her ass in the air and wiggling with each step. She turned and faced us. "I'm asking if I can watch."

I did like to be part of the show. I pulled back the sheets to expose myself. I finished the job my cock had started in working itself free from my boxers, and fisted it loosely. "Like this?"

"Exactly like that." Daria looked at Colin. "Yes or no?"

He kicked aside the bedding as well and pushed down the waistband of his shorts to expose himself. "Yes."

Fuck yes. I focused on Daria since the show was for her. The way she watched us with her tongue caught between her teeth and her chest heaving with every breath. As I stroked slowly, she kneaded her breasts through her tank top, then worked one free.

Watching her watching us was hotter than most things my imagination could come up with, especially knowing Colin was part of the same show.

She moved her hand lower, to press through her shorts.

That wouldn't do at all. "Take them off," I ordered. "I want to see your gorgeous pussy."

Daria's blush spread down her neck and to her exposed breast and nipple. So alluring. She pushed off her bottoms, lay back halfway with her weight on one arm to prop her up, and spread her legs. The way she danced her fingers along her slick, glistening skin made me groan.

"So fucking stunning." I stroked faster, and couldn't help watch for a moment as Colin did the same, his fist sliding up and down his thick, hard cock. I forced my attention back to Daria. "What do I have to do from here to get you off?"

She shook her head. "I'm not the show."

"Aren't you?" I tightened my grip and my body reacted, desire mounting inside.

Daria bit her bottom lip and dipped her fingers lower, sliding inside herself, before drawing her touch back up.

"Fuck, Daria." I needed to slow down or this would be over too soon. Or speed her up. "I want to see you come. See your gorgeous expression. Hear your incredible voice."

The way her gaze never left me as she circled her clit, the way she focused on my cock, as she rubbed herself faster, had me clenching to keep from finishing.

Her eyelids fluttered and her lips parted with a loud sigh. Her breath came in short pants.

Colin's grunts overlapped her gasps, and I could picture him jerking off to this same show.

Daria's cries when she came were better than the music last night. I swore I could feel her fingers on me, teasing my skin. She shuddered away and slowed to a stop, but she never pulled her eyes from me.

Colin let out a series of punctuated grunts that blended into a long groan, and I knew he had finished too.

I was done. I closed my eyes and tilted my head as I stopped trying to hold back. Orgasm spilled through me and stars danced behind my eyes. My pulse whined in my ears. I squeezed and pumped until my fist was a sticky mess and my dick ached.

I collapsed against the headboard with a strained laugh, and forced my eyes open. I looked between Colin and Daria. Each of them was flushed and stunning in their post coital bliss. "Number one best morning of my life," I said.

Colin's smile was lazy. "That's a high bar."

"I know what I said." As the words passed my lips a thought flashed in my mind. Could I go back to what life was before this?

Of course I could. That was the plan, that was the only option. It wouldn't be a problem.

15
daria

Last night I was almost party to a major fuck-up. I let my desire get in the way of reason, and I wouldn't have forgiven myself if Colin and Tanner lost their friendship because of it.

Sure, they were adults and making their own decisions, but I'd pushed in a direction I shouldn't have.

But waking up between them for a second morning in a row, both of them obviously erect, was hard for me to ignore.

Things were good after, though. That was what mattered. We all showered, no one was avoiding anyone else, and they both helped me move everything out of the living room, so the carpet cleaners could come and fix my mess from last night.

Colin and Tanner headed out to do their own things, and I was left alone with my thoughts and my short to-do list. Tanner did promise he'd be back early this afternoon to help with that, but for now, what was I supposed to do?

My phone ringing was a welcome distraction. The screen said it was Carly and I had *so much* to tell her.

"Hey, girl," I answered. "Welcome back."

"Hey." Carly's voice was all sunshine and confidence. "Got your message. Wanted to say *hi*. Find out why you're not in Hawaii."

I was dying to tell her every last detail, but I had no idea where to start. "Eh, you know. Bernie. But I'm done with that, so I'm chilling. How was Italy?" I didn't need to provide details; she knew enough to fill in the blanks.

"Same as always. Gorgeous. Enviable. Calling my name." Carly spent enough time there that she had talked several times about moving. I was both surprised and grateful she hadn't yet. "You let that asshole talk you into missing a week on the beach?"

"I'd rather take the trip with the girls"—and what was happening here was way better than sand in my buttcrack and a mediocre hookup with a stranger—"so it's fine."

"Fine? This was supposed to be your vacation and it's *fine*? Hair is fine. Ranch dressing on salad is fine. Time off should at least be *good*, or some more fabulous adjective. Wait. Sexy swim coaches are still staying at your place, yes or no?"

I laughed as heat carried on memories flooded through me. "Yes." I had to tell her. I was dying to talk about this and hadn't realized until she asked.

"And Oh. My. God." That summed the experience up nicely.

"Whoa. Back the fuck up," Carly said. "Eye candy doesn't get that kind of reaction. You were going to gloss over whatever led to a statement like that with *fine*? The fuck, Daria?"

"It's a story best told in person." And I needed to wrap my head around words for the last few nights that went beyond *hubba hubba*.

Carly huffed. "Fine. Mimosas at Mia's, one hour. You bring details, I'll bring presents. *Mwah*." She disconnected.

I had no idea how I was going to sum this up, but I did like tripping back through the memories in order to figure it out.

I stuck around the house long enough to let the cleaners in. Steve, the guy who ran the company and who was overseeing this cleaning personally, was a long-time friend. I didn't have a problem handing him the keys to the house, telling him to lock up when he was done, and being on my way to meet Carly.

She was already waiting outside the restaurant when I got there. We asked for a table outside, placed our orders, and sent the waitress on her way.

As soon as we were alone, Carly leaned in. "Spill. Now. I go on a boring, normal trip to Milan, and you manage to live a romance novel meet cute while I'm gone, plus turn it filthy."

"It's not a romance novel and it's not cute." I was

being intentionally vague, and enjoying drawing this out just a little.

"*Fine.*" Carly huffed. "A porn script then. Are they still hot when you spend more than a few hours at a time with them?"

I smiled. "They're fine."

She laughed. "You kill me, babe. Sexy swimmers. Younger men. Temporary roommates in awkward situations with implausible tangents. And dirty sex. I'll deny ever saying this, but I'm positively green right now. *Envy.*"

"I never said it was dirty." I paused. "I mean, it totally was, but you can't just assume."

"Touché," Carly said. "So it was good?"

I sipped my drink slowly, letting her question hang in the air as I pretended to consider my answer.

Carly pursed her lips and drummed perfectly manicured nails on the table. She checked her watch. She let out a sigh. "*Daria.*"

I laughed. "I think my earlier statement of *oh my God* sums up the situation well. No other words. Except maybe *bow-chica-bow-wow.*"

"I'm pretty sure you're glowing."

"I'm having so much fun. And I know it's only for a few days, but they're so…" I really was having a hard time describing this without gushing like a schoolgirl. "It's everything you'd want a setup like this to be, but wouldn't dare hope for. They put the dishes in the dishwasher the other night, Carly. One of them helped me vacuum."

Carly snorted. "But there's sex too, right? I mean, if you want gorgeous hunks of man meat to do the housework, there are services for that."

"But they did it because they *wanted* to. And yes, I already told you, there's sex too."

"*Boom.*" Carly leaned back in her seat with a grin. "I'm such a proud friend right now. Jealous as fuck, but good for you."

I loved that she was for this rather than judging me. Not that judgmental had ever been an issue with Carly, but not everyone could have the best best friend in the world. "Don't let me steal the entire morning. I want to know about this property in Italy."

"It's gorgeous. We literally don't have anything like it here because it's five hundred years old. The stonework, the stained glass, the wooden beams..." She grabbed her phone, made a few swipes, then passed it across the table.

I scrolled through a few dozen images. Carly could tell me what every bit of architecture was called, and what time periods this was from or mimicked. To me, it was simply gorgeous. Originally it was a cathedral that had become many other things over the centuries. Kandace was mentoring a pair of men who wanted to turn it into a high-end restaurant, then spin out similar concepts from there, across Europe.

One of the reasons I loved working for The Raphael Group was they weren't just angel investors. Some of the partners mentored people who had what could be a fantastic success, but didn't necessarily have the know-how to build a proposal and pitch it to an investment group.

I handed her phone back. "You're giving it a thumbs up?"

"Absolutely. You know what you should do, since you canceled your trip—head out there with me in a few months, and check on things."

That sounded like a lot of fun. "That would mean bringing the girls." Which sounded like fun to me, but Carly was childless by choice, and not always the biggest fan of kids.

"Your kids are well-behaved, so it's all good. So much good food. The art. The buildings... Now's the time to do this."

It was a trip I'd wanted to take for a while. "We'll see."

"I just put your *yes* in my calendar." Carly grinned.

"*Oh*, speaking of buildings and sexy swimmers, I need a favor."

She stared at me, brow furrowed, then shook her head. "I want a comeback for that, but I've got nothing. What's up?"

"Tanner is looking at a building, and he's getting conflicting information about whether it's good or not. Give it a look for him? For me?"

"All right. I need a week or two, but no problem."

We chatted a lot longer, said our goodbyes, and I headed home. As I walked inside, the heavy smell of perfumed deodorizer and wet greeted me. So much better than the toxic situation I'd left down here last night.

The note on the kitchen table from Steve said to stay off the carpet as much as possible today, and that it should be okay by tomorrow morning.

Damn. I'd probably be best off asking the guys to stay in my room again tonight… if they were okay with it. The thought pasted a goofy smile on my face and sent butterflies dancing in my tummy.

My phone rang and I grabbed it without thought. "This is Daria."

"Why the hell aren't you answering your emails? Why does your chat show you offline?" Bernie's harsh questions shattered my mood.

My instinct was to shirk away from his anger, but I didn't do that with business associates or anyone. Besides, I wasn't in the wrong. "I spoke with Kandace, and she ordered me to take the rest of the week off once the fire was out."

"*Kandace* didn't secure your time for the week." Bernie's sneer was like nails on a chalkboard. "You're working on my project, and I offered you an incredible bonus to do so."

He'd offered a reasonable bonus considering the request, but I wouldn't argue the subjective. "The work is done. I didn't leave the task unfinished."

"Your week was mine. That was our agreement. This is absolutely unacceptable."

What was I supposed to say? I could offer to be available for the next day and a half, but my anger was rising at his tone and approach, and that made me want to say *fuck you* and hang up. "What do you propose?" I resisted the urge to ask the question through gritted teeth.

"I propose you wipe your machine of any and all company information, and don't come back on Monday."

My heart stopped. I'd heard him wrong, I must have. "Excuse me?"

"I'm terminating your employment with the company, effective immediately. Expect paperwork this afternoon. Enjoy your extended vacation, Ms. Lane."

The line went dead.

I stared at my phone, and numbness spread through my veins. What in the... That didn't... What?

16
tanner

TODAY WAS A GOOD DAY.

Who was I kidding? Today was an incredible day. From the way it started—mutual masturbation in bed was *way* better than breakfast in bed. Could I call that breakfast in bed? To the fact that I'd made my target time at the pool. Multiple times in a row. I was heading to the qualifying trials for the Olympics in a month.

I'd shouted, I'd yelled, I'd punched the air, and I'd even done a dance at the edge of the pool. I wished Colin was there to celebrate with me, but we could figure that out tonight.

He was right to stop me last night. I hadn't been thinking clearly. Now that I'd had a chance today, I was good with it. With kissing him and if it turned into more. Not that we had many more days here to play, but we might as well continue to enjoy our not-vacation.

When I stepped into Daria's house, I wasn't surprised to see portions of the living room still crammed into the dining room. It was the way the cushions from the couch were configured that made me pause. Some were stacked on their ends, and others sat on the table, pinning a blanket in place that was draped over chairs and more cushions.

Was there a blanket fort in the dining room?

I didn't hear anyone talking, and the only car outside was Daria's, so the carpet cleaners were probably gone. I approached the structure quietly. "Daria?"

"Yeah." Her voice was soft, and it definitely came from under the blankets.

"Can I come in?" Did I really just ask that? This was surreal.

"Sure."

I knelt, and crawled through what could be a doorway, where two blankets overlapped.

Daria was sitting inside, knees pulled to her chest, clutching a stuffed duck in a pink sweater.

Excitement was making me hallucinate? I kept the thought to myself—the mood in the air felt far more somber than that. "Who's your friend?" I asked instead.

"Mr. Garibaldi."

I didn't get it. "Interesting name for a duck."

She studied me. "Obvious name for a duck."

"If you say so."

"Never let Dustin know you don't get that reference. You'll be watching B5 for a week, and he'll make sure of it."

I'd only met Dustin a few times, and only in passing when he dropped Alana off for practice. The way Daria casually tossed the comment out there, as if a conversation like that was likely to come up in the future, warmed me in a way I didn't expect. "I'll keep that in mind."

I made my way completely into the tent-slash-cave, and sat across from her. "Roomy for a tiny home. Sits two comfortably."

"I know what I'm doing. Sometimes. I thought I did." She frowned and squeezed the duck tightly. "You don't need to hear about that. How was your day?"

It was incredible. I wasn't the one who needed to be listened to. "What happened?"

"Nothing. Not a big deal."

Except a grown ass woman who I had never seen falter for more than a heartbeat, who always wore an air of having her shit together, had built herself a pillow fort and was squeezing the stuffing out of Mr. Ghirardelli as if he were her lifeline. "I hear it helps if you talk about it."

She let out a bitter laugh and cut it off with the shake of her head. "I was just fired. That's all."

"I'm sorry." That wasn't the right answer. I should be asking why or how I could help or furious. That last one felt the most right, even without information. No one should—

"I'm still numb," she said. "But that's wearing off. You know how after the dentist, you can't feel your lips, and then you know the Novocain is wearing off because there's a tingle, but it doesn't go away all at once and you know when it does it's going to hurt and it's this creeping sensation you want to prod at anyway, and just get to the pain faster?"

I nodded. Several responses tumbled to my lips but the *just listen* was the loudest voice in my head.

"I'm good at my job. I'm incredible at what I do. And it doesn't matter. And then I think about all those nights I told Alana *maybe tomorrow* or begged her to read Harmony a bedtime story so I could finish *just one more thing.*" Daria drew in a shuddering breath. "Because it would be better *tomorrow*. Because I had to work. For us.

"And now it doesn't matter. Those assholes don't care what I sacrificed. They only remember that *one fucking time when I was supposed to be on vacation* and I wasn't at their beck and call. I know I'll land on my feet, but I gave up so much. Why?" She looked at me as she asked the question, as if I might have more insight into her pain than she did.

I still remembered how much it hurt when I tore my rotator cuff at the Olympics. Not just physically, but the anguish I let myself wallow in over *why*? My heart had hurt for... I wasn't sure it ever completely stopped.

I could tell her that. Use it as a basis for *I understand.*

But I also still remembered Colin helping me climb out of the depths of that pit, and how intently he'd always listened and only nudged when I needed a reply or a kick in the ass.

This felt more like the first one. "You've always done what you thought was right and best. That's the most anyone can ask for."

"But it wasn't. I wasn't. I missed so much."

"But you didn't." I wasn't just saying that to comfort her. " I hear the kids talk and I see how they interact with their parents. I know which moms and dads are going to hit on either Colin or me, and which parents we've never met because they always sent their kids to practice—to meets—with someone else. I know who berates, who brushes off, or barely glances at their children."

Daria's mouth was drawn in a straight line. "I assume you're going somewhere with this."

I was. "And I've never seen you do any of those things. You make it to every meet, even if it means coming home in the middle of a business trip. Alana and Harmony think the world of you. Harmony tells everyone her mom is the best mom in the world. And Alana never joins in the bitching about parents. And I realize there are things no one sees, behind closed doors, but... you put down sexy pillow fight time the instant they called last night."

"Technically sexy pillow fight time never happened, and we'd already moved on." Some of the shadows had faded from Daria's expression, though.

I stretched my legs out in front of me and patted my thigh. She lay her head on my leg, still clutching the duck.

The silence was strange, but it wasn't uncomfortable. I moved my hand, not aware of what I was doing until I touched her scalp, but she didn't protest or try to pull away as I trailed my fingers through her hair.

Daria really was all those things I'd said, and more. She was this amazing woman I had so much respect for, and she looked so lost and vulnerable right now. That made her even more human and even more amazing, that she could be both.

I lost track of how long we sat there for. This was so simple. I'd never had this kind of closeness with anyone.

Except Colin.

The tiny disconnect—that I wanted this kind of intimacy from both of them—would fry my brain if I let it. That wasn't fair to anyone, and I couldn't dwell on the thought because right now wasn't about me.

"You need to be pampered for the rest of the day," I said softly.

Her dry chuckle surprised me. "I appreciate the sentiment." She sat up and looked at me. "But that's not what I need right now. Grab your laptop, I'll clean off the table."

"What?"

"You heard me."

"You're allowed to take the time to deal with this."

Daria shook her head. "I need to feel wanted." She snapped her jaw shut. "I mean... I need to be doing something and you have a business proposal to make sparkle and shine."

An impulse raged inside to wrap her up, kiss her hard, and tell her I'd always want her.

Where the fuck did that come from?

It didn't matter because she wouldn't take a statement like that seriously. Besides, this wasn't about sex, and I understood where she was coming from because I felt the same way after my injury.

"Okay. I'll be right back." I grasped her fingertips and brushed my lips over her knuckles.

No, really, what was I doing? It was a good thing I had Daria's crisis to focus on because I had no idea what was going on in my own head.

17
colin

I WOULD'VE WRAPPED up the mural at the antique shop yesterday if Deacon hadn't needed to close up early. Which meant it didn't take long to finish the work once I arrived.

Barely enough time to linger on thoughts of last night. Way too much time to over-analyze Tanner's kisses and decisions and his choosing to stop.

Sure, I told him to.

But lump that decision into the over thinking bucket as well and I could call it a massive mess.

Those thoughts would wait. I stepped back to take a bigger picture look at my work. It wasn't perfect— as the artist, I saw every flaw and mistake—but hopefully Deacon would call it good enough.

"Holy shit. That's amazing." His comment caught me off-guard. I hadn't realized he was there.

I wouldn't correct his perception; I learned a long time ago the customer saw things in a different light than I did when it came to my work. "Thanks. I'm calling it done, but if you see anything you'd like touched up or tweaked, I can do it."

"No way." He stepped up next to me. "I thought you were done a few hours ago, but each new detail… man you brought this to life."

The praise was nice. The paycheck would be good too. I pulled out my phone. "You okay with me taking a few pictures and adding them to my portfolio?"

"Yeah, of course."

I took some close-ups of some of the more detailed work, then stepped back to get some wide angles. Deacon insisted on taking a few of me in front of the work as well, to post on his website.

"Seriously, incredible work. Brooke told me you were good, but you know."

I did. "Sisters are biased."

"Exactly. She undersold you, though. Hey, let me buy you a coffee, to celebrate a job well done."

I hadn't forgotten how heavily Deacon leaned into the flirting a few days ago. If I accepted his offer, would I be encouraging more of the same? And was it a big deal if I did? I was wild and free and having one-night stands. Sure, they meant more to me than they should, and I was going to deal with that. This was me loosening up.

"Just this once." I kept my tone light and teasing.

Deacon and I headed across the street, grabbed our drinks, and took a spot in the back of the cafe,

Allyson Lindt

away from late morning chatter and early lunch stragglers.

He scooted his chair closer, so his knee touched mine when he leaned in. "Million-dollar question, how did you get into something like mural painting?"

It wasn't a big grand story, but it was something only and Tanner and Brooke knew, because most people never asked. "I went through a wild patch when I was younger. I was pissed off that I got shit for liking guys, but also for still liking girls. Like both sides hated me. So I expressed myself through painting."

I'd much rather be telling Daria this story. The thought surprised me. But I'd finish sharing with Deacon since I'd already started.

"I get that." Deacon sounded sincere and sympathetic. "I'm sorry you had to deal with it. But *murals*. Why so big?"

This was the part of the story I kept to myself. "I was a tagger. Graffiti artist. I left my signature everywhere, in the form of pictures. If the world didn't want to see me, I was going to force them to."

"Wow." Deacon radiated awe.

I shook my head. "It's not that impressive. The murals were a way to cover up the vandalism."

Deacon chuckled. "Talented. Rebellious. Contentious. Sexy." He covered my hand and his gaze drifted toward my crotch. "You really are the full package."

And there was the not-subtle-at-all flirting again. I

couldn't do this. I wanted Tanner and Daria. I wanted more and more of the last two nights. Hooking up with someone else would either add another name to the *I can't control my crushes* list, or more likely be a lie to myself and Deacon. "Listen, you're a great guy…"

"Whoa." Deacon pulled his hand away. "I know that tone. Are you about to friendzone me before we even become friends?"

I winced. "I'm about to be honest with you. I think we could be friends, but you're not going to get more from me."

"Huh." Deacon scooted his seat back to where it had been, but he looked thoughtful rather than upset. "Yeah. Okay."

That was disturbingly easy. "Just like that?"

"I dunno." He shrugged. "I like the honesty. It's sexy." He frowned. "And friendly. And now I know, so I won't push myself on you, and you don't have to feel weird around me."

Oh. Weird, but nice.

"So now what?" Deacon asked.

"Well, you can cut me a check and pretend we never met, or I can stay and we can finish our coffee." Would I be having a conversation like this with Daria in a few days? With Tanner? *It was amazing sex, but let's just go back to what we were.*

As easy as the conversation went with Deacon, the idea of saying something like that Tanner or Daria soured in my stomach.

"Let's stay." Deacon leaned back in his seat. "You

can ask me the one thing you've been dying to since you showed up that first day."

There was a question. "You get this one a lot?"

"Only from the perceptive people."

"All right, the acronym for your shop…"

Deacon laughed. "Triple D. Yeah, it's on purpose, and while I put a lot of thought into it, it's not one of my finer decisions."

"Because you're all about the D?" I sipped my coffee. This was simple. Fun. No pressure. I liked it.

"Nah," Deacon said. "I mean, yes, but also, like you, I'm more into the *why limit myself* idea. I'll take a pair of nice double D's, or a D, whatever."

"I…" Words failed me.

Deacon tilted his head and studied me. "I think you're blushing."

"I think I'm both impressed and disturbed by your dedication to the hidden crudeness."

"You have your art, I have mine," Deacon said.

I laughed and shook my head. We talked a bit longer, he paid me, and I was on my way.

The conversation I'd had with him, the directness, that was exactly what I needed to do with Tanner. What I'd put off for way too long. I was going to do it —tell Tanner how I felt as soon as this week was over.

Though, did that push Daria out of our lives? What if it pushed Tanner away?

It didn't matter. Rather, it did, but dragging things out in fear of an answer I didn't want to hear wasn't doing any of us any favors.

When I got back to the house, I was surprised to find Daria and Tanner at the kitchen table, crowded in between cushions and smaller furniture, both of them with their laptops up.

Tanner looked up, and grinned. "Grab your sketchpad. We need your help."

"With what?" I was going to do it anyway, but I was curious.

"I need to take my mind off the fact that I was fired."

I stared at Daria in disbelief. "I heard you wrong. Something was on fire?"

"You heard me right. My asshole ex-boss decided that he didn't like me not working on my vacation, and he let me go."

"He can't do that." I didn't try to hide my anger on her behalf. "You've got legal recourse. You could sue his ass off. What kind of an idiot lets a talent like yours go?"

Amusement danced in her eyes, but it clashed with her sadness. "I've been thinking about the legal thing pretty much since I got the news. Deciding if I wanted to pursue it or if I want to move on. Both, I suppose. I don't want to move on from the company, but I do want to cut ties with the asshole who fired me. And I want him to never do something like that to someone else again."

"Good," Tanner said. "I could also go punch him, if you want."

"I do, but don't do that." Daria huffed out a short

laugh. "But all the lawyers I know are because of the firm, so they can't help me. Conflict of interest."

How different would it be to have the kind of business contacts where one could casually say *all the lawyers I know*... but that wasn't the point. "Brooke worked with a great divorce lawyer," I offered.

Daria frowned and worked her jaw.

"I understand divorce is not employment law, or whatever it's called, but I bet she can get a name for you. I'll ask her."

"Thank you. For everything." Daria looked between us.

Tanner typed a few things on his laptop and looked up. "Because letting you fix our business plan and Colin calling his sister are such rough tasks."

"It's the thought that counts."

I'd never heard someone say that with so much sincerity. "You're worth it."

Daria blushed. "Go get your sketchpad. We need your genius to pull this all together."

"Done." I set my portfolio case on the ground, unzipped it, and pulled out the notebook in question, along with my favorite drafting pencil. "What are we doing?"

Tanner toed the chair closest to him toward me. "We need visuals for the remodels you would do to the rec center if you could. Not just the pool, but the classrooms and gym."

I grinned and set to work. Tanner had mentioned the rest of the building, but his approach was so vague, I hadn't put much stock in it. Today he had a grander vision, that I suspected Daria had helped him expand on. And I didn't mind at all.

While I sketched, we also discussed activities for the kids who weren't swimming, bringing on other instructors, and me offering a lot of feedback on how I thought it should all work.

It was incredible. I could see the project coming to life in a way I hadn't for a long time.

We worked our way through the Chinese food leftovers, and Daria made cookies while we planned.

"I feel a little spoiled." I meant it in the kindest way. "You're doing all of this for us, plus cookies?"

She waved a hand. "Don't be too impressed. I keep a tub of cookie dough in the fridge, and I would have eaten it raw, in a fit of frustration, if the two of you weren't here to keep me busy."

The whisper of sadness in her voice was obvious, but she moved on to the next subject before I could push the issue.

It was almost eight at night when we finished, but Tanner and I had a fully revised business plan and I felt great about the future of the project. Of everything, really.

"I'd prefer to keep out of the living room for one more night, since the carpet is still damp," Daria said.

I liked where the thought was going. "We'd probably better stay in your room again tonight, if that's the case."

Tanner clapped me on the shoulder. "What did I tell you? Idea guy, right here."

I was grinning as I put away my sketchpad. I knocked a box loose, and it clattered to the floor.

"What's that?" Daria asked as I reached for it.

Tanner got to it first. "Edible body paint?"

I shrugged. "It was a gag gift, and I've never figured out what to do with it. It's paint, so it goes with the paint supplies." Probably a good thing that was knocked loose here, and not at Deacon's. Inspiration struck. "I have the perfect idea for it now, though."

"You're on a roll tonight," Tanner said. "Do tell."

This was the point where I should put a pause on things and say *hey, where's all of this going between the three of us after this week?* But I wasn't in the mood to ruin this moment. I fixed my gaze on Daria. "I have the perfect canvas in mind."

18
daria

WHEN COLIN SAID he had the perfect canvas for his paints, my pulse kicked up in anticipation. My brain hadn't caught up to why, until Colin looked at me.

"Tell me Daria doesn't have the perfect body for a mural," he said.

Tanner dragged his gaze over me. "She really does."

Heat flooded my body. "I don't..."

"You can say no." Colin was really so sweet.

That wasn't my issue, though. "I want to say *yes*, I just don't know how body painting works."

"We need an old sheet or towels for the bed. Something you don't mind staining," Tanner said.

Colin nodded. "Then you strip down so I can do the actual painting."

"Then we get to appreciate the final artwork." Tanner made it sound so simple and obvious.

The spark of desire pooling in my belly and traveling lower thought it was anything but simple. I loved the idea, though.

If we were in a porn, the cut would have taken us past the next few minutes of trooping up the stairs, finding an old comforter, and covering the bed. How did such a simple but awkward series of actions raise my desire even higher?

Standing in my bedroom with Tanner and Colin, heat spilling through me, was already becoming addictively familiar. Tanner studied me with a playful smirk as he fiddled with the button on my jeans. I didn't get the impression he was struggling so much as having fun.

Colin tugged my shirt over my head, and kissed along my bare shoulder. "Absolutely perfect canvas." As he unhooked my bra, Tanner pushed my jeans and panties to the ground.

Standing in the middle of my own room naked felt weird. They'd seen me without my clothes, but this was different. We weren't wrapped up in kissing and groping, and my stretch marks and less than perky breasts and cesarean scar were all on display.

I hugged myself, suddenly self-conscious.

Tanner tugged one of my arms down. "What's wrong?"

"This feels strange."

"We can't have that. What do you propose?"

I only saw one real solution. "That I'm not the only naked one."

"The artist usually keeps his clothes on." Colin

traced a finger along my arm. "But I think it's a fair request."

There was nothing fancy about the way they stripped out of their clothes, but I enjoyed watching it as much as I'd liked having it done to me. And staring at them naked in their full glory took my mind off my own nudity.

Colin walked a small circle around me, raking his gaze over me in a way that was as delicious as any touch. "I think I need you standing for this." He handed the paints to Tanner. "My trusty assistant will help me."

I expected Tanner to protest the term. Instead, he opened the red paint, dipped his finger in, and dragged the color in a vertical strip down my bottom lip and chin. He dragged his tongue over the stripe, licking the color away before pressing his mouth to mine.

"Is it cherry flavored?" I asked against his kiss.

He drew away. "It's red flavored. It's you flavored. It's my new favorite flavor."

And now I was probably completely red, without any more paint.

"I'll draw the lines, you fill them in?" Colin looked at Tanner.

Tanner grinned. "With pleasure."

A shiver of anticipation raced down my spine.

Colin used his fingers to draw a series of flowing lines that became vines and roses. He trailed along my breasts and stomach, around my thighs, and back up again. Each stroke was cool paint mixed with the heat of his touch.

While he moved in effortless creation, Tanner's lingering on the details made me want to squeeze my thighs together. That would have stopped Colin's progress though.

The longer they spent *painting* me, the harder it was to not squirm. Especially seeing them both erect, their cocks brushing me each time one of them leaned in.

When they finished, they both stepped back.

"Absolutely stunning." The way Tanner looked me over, I felt like a statue of a Greek goddess. "So's the art, my friend."

Colin looked smug. "Told you. *Perfect* canvas."

"Even better, you're edible." Tanner pressed two paint covered fingers to my lips.

I pulled them into my mouth and dragged my tongue along the pads, sucking him clean. His throaty groan and the way his eyelids fluttered half open cranked my desire higher.

He dragged his fingers down my chin, following the same path with a line of kisses, licking when he reached the paint along my collarbone.

Colin dropped his head to trace his tongue along one breast. He drew a nipple into his mouth and sucked.

The two of them spent more time licking me clean than they had painting me, occasionally drifting closer to share a spot, their tongues tangling with each other. By the time they reached my thighs, my pussy was begging for attention.

Tanner kissed back up my hip and to my back, until he was nipping at my neck, and sucking on the soft skin where it met my shoulder. He slipped two fingers between my legs, teasing over my skin, but not penetrating or offering relief.

Colin crushed his mouth to mine, and his erection pressed into my stomach. He followed, never breaking the kiss, when Tanner yanked my head back to expose more of my neck.

I needed something to do. To hold onto. I wrapped my hand around Colin's shaft, and his long moan undid me. If they could tease, so could I. Adjusting my stance slightly, I dragged the head of Colin's cock along my slit. When I bumped my clit, we groaned in unison.

Tanner let go of my hair, and slipped his fingers inside me, drawing a gasp from me.

A woman could only hold out for so long. I stroked Colin, using his tip to tease myself. The harder I pumped, the closer I slid to climax. He gripped my hips. His lips parted and his breathing came in short pants, matching mine, as I masturbated both of us.

Orgasm slammed into me and I clenched around Tanner's fingers, never letting up on Colin. His grunts came harder and faster. I already recognized the sound of his mounting release. When he came, he covered my hand, my body.

I slowed to a stop as we both shuddered from *too much*, and he claimed my mouth again as if we were each other's lifelines.

"Fuck." Tanner's exclamation rumbled through my back. He slipped out of me, and reached past me to grip Colin's neck. I moved aside enough to not get caught in their kiss.

Colin met Tanner's gaze with an unspoken question that charged the air, and I swore Tanner's faint nod was a spark that lit up the room. Colin kissed down Tanner's chest, already fisting his cock.

And I made myself comfortable on the old bedspread, to enjoy every minute of the show.

19

tanner

I was drowning. Gasping for air, and Colin and Daria were my lifelines. His mouth. Her hungry gaze. I needed both to stay afloat.

Colin dragged his lips down my chest, and nipped his teeth over one of my nipples before flicking the nub with his tongue.

I didn't know where one groan stopped and the next started, but I did know I was rock hard.

And then he was on knees in front of me, looking up at me with eyes I could fall into forever.

I knotted my fingers in the short strands of his hair in response. This was sex between friends, and I was going to enjoy the hell out of it.

He lightly trailed his tongue along my cock. *Fuuu-uuck.* I was so turned on, I almost came when he took me in his mouth.

Colin teased me with a slow, steady blend of licking, sucking, and stroking. Between it all, he fingered my sac.

This was incredible, but I was past the point of wanting to draw things out. I tightened my grip on his hair, and thrust my hips.

Colin responded with enthusiasm, not protesting when I hit the back of his throat, and bobbing his head as I fucked his face.

Need clenched inside me, tightening in my balls. I wanted this to last longer, but I also wanted that sweet release. "I'm so close." I managed to grunt out the words.

My warning seemed to spur Colin on. His hunger combined with Daria's soft moans to yank and break my last threads of restraint.

I closed my eyes and leaned back my head. Light exploded behind my eyelids when I came, leaving stars dancing in my vision. I spilled down Colin's throat, pumping until every touch was too much before I finally forced myself to pull away.

Daria shifted on the bed, lying on her stomach as she kissed Colin hard.

I watched with aching desire as they shared my taste. *Fuck* that was delicious to watch.

When the two of them broke apart, all three of us collapsed on the bed, Daria and Colin curling up on either side of me. We lay there for I didn't even know how long, catching our breath. When we finally untangled enough to clean up, the washcloth I traced along Daria's skin didn't lift off the lingering traces of body paint.

"It doesn't matter." Her tiny smile seemed fixed in place. *Stunning.* "It'll fade in a few days, and until then, I'll remember now every time I see it."

"I hope you'll remember anyway," I teased.

Her laugh was musical. "I don't think I'll ever forget."

We reluctantly dressed, and Daria decided that with the old blanket already in place, it was the perfect time to eat popcorn in bed and watch more Game of Thrones.

As we were settling in, the heavenly smell of butter and salt in the air, my good news from earlier rushed back. "I almost forgot."

"That we need ice cream?" Daria asked.

I glanced at Colin, who shrugged, so I looked at Daria again. "With the popcorn or after?"

She grinned. "It's a thing Harmony does. She says *I almost forgot,* and when you ask what, she says *we should have ice cream.*"

That was freaking adorable. And something about the casual way Daria shared the memory felt intimate, as if we were part of her family. I liked it. "I'm in for ice cream, but that's not what I was talking about. I made my time this morning. I'm going to the Olympic trials in a few weeks to see if I can make the team."

"*Yeah.*" Colin clapped me on the back. "I can see it now, painted under our school's name. *Featuring*

Olympic Medalist…" He wiped his hand across the air as he spoke.

I was as pleased with his reaction as I was with my news. He was into the school idea again, and that was perfect.

"You'll have to send us postcards," Daria said. "Alana desperately wants to go to Tokyo, and I've told her not until Harmony is older."

"I promise, lots of postcards."

We settled in to watch the show, and like last night we had an amazing time laughing and both enjoying and making fun of what was happening.

I didn't want this to end. It had to though. After this week, this would be a memory and nothing more. So for tonight, I was memorizing it.

THREE NIGHTS in a row of some of the most fun I'd ever had. The sex was incredible, but the company was amazing regardless.

And waking up in the same bed as Daria and Colin was my new favorite way to start a morning.

Colin and I made Daria stay in bed, and made her breakfast. We took our time feeding each other strawberries and regretting that I hadn't poured the juice into sippy cups, when we had to leave it on the nightstand, and just enjoying each other's company.

I didn't want this to end, but after tomorrow, Colin

and I would be back in our place and life would go back to normal.

I might as well enjoy it all now, while I could.

A creak from downstairs greeted us, and Daria jerked upright with a frown. "That was the front door."

Where was the nearest weapon?

"*Mom.*" Alana's call carried easily up the stairs. "We're home."

"Fuck me." Panic flooded Daria's expression.

No kidding. Colin and I were on our feet in an instant, pulling on clothes, tossing Daria her T-shirt, and making the bed look at least a little like only one person had been sleeping in it.

At the sound of the bedroom doorknob turning, nausea surged in my gut. At least we were all decent when Alana walked in the room.

She froze, eyes wide and mouth open, then let out the most painful, ear-splitting screech I'd ever heard.

20
colin

IN FRONT OF DARIA'S, Tanner made a quick call to the apartment management office and made sure we were okay to go back to our apartment. With confirmation, we headed *home.*

I arrived there about the same time he did. It hadn't even been five days, but it felt weird coming back here. Inside the apartment, the faint smell of something peppery hung in the air, and we opened the windows immediately.

Neither of us had said much of anything. Was his mind racing as much as mine was? "I hope Daria's all right," I finally said.

Tanner fidgeted with his fingers, rubbing them together. "She's never mentioned that her ex was abusive. Neither has Alana. Do you think she might be in trouble? We shouldn't have left. If he hurts her…"

His concern was adorable and as far as I knew,

completely misplaced. "I meant emotionally, you neanderthal. She looked so stressed."

"I know." Tanner sighed and sank onto the couch. "And did you hear that scream of Alana's?"

"She's going to hate us forever." I didn't like the thought of having disappointed a student. I really didn't like thinking about the tension in that house when we left. And the things her ex had been saying to her... This was one of those rare moments when I understood why someone might punch someone else.

Tanner was on his feet again, pacing the short distance of the living room. "I need to do something."

We'd walked out of Daria's with our wallets, keys, and phones. Our laptops were still there, and a week's worth of clothing. There was one thing I wanted to do. Well, two, but the second was probably driven by stress and may happen after the first. After I was finally honest with Tanner about how I felt.

As I opened my mouth, my phone rang. Daria's name flashed on the screen. "Thank God," I muttered, and answered. "Are you all right?"

Tanner fixed his attention on me with the question, and his feet stopped moving.

"I'm fine." Daria's voice leaked stress. "Will you give this same message to Tanner?"

"Of course." I'd offer to put her on speaker, but there was a reason she called me.

She sighed. "You can come pick up your things anytime, just give me ten minutes warning. And..." Another sigh, that sounded like her trying to exhale the weight of the world. "This week was so much fun, but things need to go back to the way they were. We can't do things like that anymore."

"Is this because of Joe?" I winced as the question passed my lips, and Tanner clenched his jaw. "I didn't mean that. I'm sorry."

"It's fine." She had gone from stressed to sounding flat. "And no, it's because of the girls. I can't disrupt their lives like that."

We won't be a disruption. Your kids are awesome. But that implied a commitment that went beyond what we had. "I understand. We'll text you before we come by, and it'll probably be later today."

"Let me talk to her," Tanner growled.

Not sure that was a good idea.

"It was fun. Bye." Daria hung up.

I stared at my phone. This was always going to happen. Maybe not in this way, but there was no universe where we did anything but went our separate ways at the end of the way. I'd wanted more so badly though, that I'd convinced myself otherwise. My mistake.

At the self-confession, an empty pit opened up in my heart. What did I think was going to happen though? That we'd move in with Daria and be one big happy family? Because of a few days of incredible sex and other fun?

"What did she say?" Tanner's question jarred me.

I looked up, studying his face. Those gorgeous eyes I'd lost myself in more times than he'd ever realize. Those lips… *God*, it was incredible kissing him. I couldn't let him get away without telling him.

"*Colin*." His voice was more insistent. "What did she say?"

I conveyed her brief message, still having a harder time grasping the words than I wanted to.

"How could she think… There was something there with her."

Tanner's retort echoed my thoughts in a way I didn't want them to. So why did they also rub me wrong?

"I thought this was just a fling. Casual sex between three friends," I said.

"It may have started that way, but she means a lot more."

That was what I didn't like—the qualifiers. This wasn't the way I wanted to do this. I wanted to sit down and have a sweet conversation with Tanner, where I said *I love you* and he said *me too*. But this was where we were. "Was it just sex with me, or do I mean something more too?"

The way Tanner stared at me made my gut sink.

"Because it meant more to me," I said. "*You* mean more to me."

"What do you…?" Tanner frowned.

Abort. Abort. But it was too late. I was The Titanic, set on course I couldn't possibly change in time, toward an iceberg that would destroy me. "It wasn't just sex to me. Not with her. Especially not with you. God, I love you Tanner. I have for years, and I didn't think you felt the same way, but after the last few days, how can you... We've known each other forever. How could you say it meant something with her but not with me?"

"Because you're—"

"Your pal? Your buddy? A man?" I didn't want to hear what he was going to say. it would hurt too much.

"You say all that like it's a bad thing. Your friendship means the world to me," Tanner said. "And yeah, the sex was incredible, and it sure as fuck turned Daria on."

Were the fumes making my head spin or was that my disbelief and self-disgust for seeing what wasn't there. "It didn't do anything for you. You dumped your load down my throat because Daria thought it was hot, and that was it?"

"I don't know what to say Colin. You're my best friend, and I'd be lost without that. I'm not even ashamed to say I love you, but not like that. This isn't romantic."

Could he hear my heart breaking? Unlikely. And as much as I wanted to yell at Tanner for being an idiot, this was my fault. I saw more than was there. What I wanted rather than what he said. He'd never lied to me.

"Colin?" The way Tanner watched me with concern gutted me further.

Was I only in this friendship hoping he'd put out, or was I here because he was my friend no matter what? "This is on me. But… I need to not be around you right now. Don't harass Daria when you go pick up your stuff."

I walked out the front door, letting it swing shut on one more call of, "*Colin.*"

That went better than I'd always feared, and not nearly as good as I hoped. Especially after these past few days. I let out a bitter laugh, and a neighbor walking her dog gave me a weird look.

Whatever.

Being alone would suck, because I'd be stuck listening to my thoughts, but where was I supposed to go that I wouldn't be reminded of Tanner?

I sent Daria a quick text saying I'd be by soon to grab my things. That couldn't be put off. As I climbed into my car, I called Brooke. The instant I heard her line pick up I said, "Please don't make any Tanner jokes."

"Good morning to you too." Brooke's greeting was cautiously chipper. "And why not?"

I took a deep breath and started the car. How best to put this? "I told him."

"And…? Oh. Oh, Colin."

The tone of my voice had definitely given me away. Good. That meant less to explain.

"I'm so sorry," Brooke said. "What can I do?"

"Tell me you need help with something. Anything. And maybe let me crash on your couch for a few days?"

"I do. You may. And how bad is this? Did you break up?"

I winced at her phrasing, and pointed my car toward Daria's.

"I didn't mean it that way," Brooke said. "How bad is it? Does a few days mean that, or is it more of an indefinite request? You're welcome regardless, but if you think you're going to be a while, you need to help me clear out my craft room."

"I'll straighten your fucking garage if it'll keep my mind busy." I didn't know anyone more driven than Brooke, besides Daria. My sister's entire life looked put together on the outside, as long as one didn't open the doors she kept locked. That was both literal and metaphorical. Not that I had a problem with either. "And I don't know how long. I didn't *break up* with him. I just need some space."

Brooke clucked. "I have plenty you can help with and you can stay as long as you want."

I *wanted* to be staying with Tanner. I wanted to be cuddled up with him right now, because he felt the same way I did, while we figured out how to help Daria and where he and I went next. But that wasn't what I was getting. "Thank you."

21

daria

HARMONY CAME DOWN around noon to ask if she could have breakfast for lunch. They were supposed to have Mickey Mouse pancakes today, and she didn't get any. Saying *yes* was the easiest decision ever.

Telling Colin and Tanner our relationship needed to go back to what it had been should have been just as simple. So why did I feel like I was giving up more than just amazing sex?

I wasn't anywhere near the artist Colin was, but a big circle of pancake with two smaller circles for ears, and banana slices plus chocolate chips for eyes, and Harmony had her Mickey Mouse pancakes. I even gave one a bow of strawberries so she'd have a Minnie.

"*Yay.*" Harmony clapped when she saw the food.

Alana was more sullen, never looking at me or saying a word. I was happy she came down at all, so I was calling it a win.

Harmony told me about every minute of Disneyland Day One as she ate. I was sad I hadn't been there, but I was glad she had the memories.

"But Mom." Harmony put down her fork and looked at me with a serious expression.

"Yes?"

"We didn't get to spend very much time at California Adventure. Alana wanted to go on more rides."

Alana rolled her eyes, pushed back from the table, and stalked upstairs. A door slammed shut.

Harmony frowned. "She didn't take her plate to the sink."

"I don't think your sister's feeling well." I winced inwardly at the tiny untruth. "You can help me with dishes. Like Cinderella."

"But you're not evil, Mom."

Bless her.

When we were done, Harmony skipped back to her room to introduce her new Dumbo stuffie to SpongeBob.

I kept myself busy with polishing my resume and sending word out through a few close friends that I was looking for new work. The tasks didn't keep me from wondering how to get Alana to talk to me, and worrying about her didn't stop me from wanting to pick up the phone and redefine things with Colin and Tanner to keep the sex in our lives.

I was horrible.

A little before five, Dustin called. "Everything all right there?" he asked when I answered.

That wasn't suspicious at all. "Why?"

"Alana called me and told me she and Harmony were coming to live with me."

Fuck. At least she hadn't called Joe.

"I thought they were supposed to be in California for a couple more days. What happened?" Dustin said.

I gave him the high-level list, keeping things extra vague around, "I slept with my house guests," and culminating with, "At least we were all dressed when Alana walked in the room." I didn't have much energy left to keep the story emotionless, and my voice cracked on those last words.

"Dar…"

"Don't." I stopped him at his kind tone. "I don't want sympathy or pity or even understanding. I fucked up."

He sighed. "You do the best you can. You do better than most."

"Not a high bar, Dustin."

"How about this, then? I'll loan you my girlfriend for the night."

I scowled at the phone. Now he was making fun of me, despite the lack of teasing in his voice. "I can't see how that's going to do anything except make the situation worse."

Dustin chuckled. "Not like that. Call Carly. Addie's already calling Luna and Reese. Go out for the night. No pressure. Just some unwinding. Leave Alana and Harmony here, and clear your head."

"Ignoring reality is what got me into this." Guilt gnawed me at the simple thought of doing what he suggested. Having fun when the world around me was falling apart? Nope.

"You're not ignoring things. You're approaching the situation from a different angle."

I couldn't.

"Are you going to sit at home and sulk instead?" Dustin's question was kind. "If Alana isn't talking to you, she may talk to me."

I did need to give Alana some space, and I needed it to not be with Joe.

"I'll spoil them while they're here. Give them too much ice cream." He was a master at walking that fine line between just enough and too much spoiling.

"They had to come home from Disneyland early, and caught their mom all but naked with two men. They need therapy, not ice cream."

"I'll give them candy, too," Dustin said.

I almost smiled. Dustin would give them positive attention, without trying to turn them against me. "I'll drop them off in a little bit." And then come back here and try to find a solution.

I headed upstairs, and knocked on Alana's door.

Nothing.

"Dustin called me. You can go to his house for the night," I called through the door.

She opened it with a scowl. "Or until I'm old enough to get my own place."

Words. I'd take words. "You know Dustin has a boyfriend and a girlfriend." Why did I take that approach? It wasn't as if Tanner and Colin were my boyfriends.

Alana's scowl deepened. "Adrienne and Phillip aren't my swim coaches, and Dustin isn't my mom. When people hook up and then break up, other people get hurt in the process."

"I don't want you to get hurt." And now my heart was breaking.

"Too late. I'll be in the car." She grabbed her backpack from behind the door, and brushed past me.

Harmony wasn't happy about being bundled off without warning for a second time today, but I let her bring Dumbo and Mr. Garibaldi with her, and that helped her feel better.

When I dropped the girls at Dustin's, Adrienne was waiting too. These days she spent most of her time either at his place or Phillip's, but I suspected all three of them would be living together sooner rather than later.

"Come on." Adrienne hooked her arm in mine and led me back to the car. "He's got this."

Dustin was the one person I wasn't worried about. "Where are we going?"

"Back to your place. You're a mess. Sorry. Not in a bad way. You need comfy clothes. A ponytail. A margarita." Adrienne wasn't great at filtering her thoughts.

I was fine with that. "I'm not sitting at home drinking."

"You're going to sit at home and sulk sober instead? We're not staying there." she said. She took my keys and phone from me. "Unlock this."

"Why?" I pressed my thumb to the bottom button on the phone anyway.

She typed on the screen, paused, and typed some more after each chime. When she was done, she handed the device back. "Carly and Reese are going to meet us there. Luna's already got plans."

"Meet us where?" I asked as Adrienne nudged me toward the passenger seat.

She slid behind the wheel. "Grumpy's."

A local sports bar-slash-family restaurant. "On a Friday night?"

"Loud enough you don't have to think if you don't want. Lots of comfort food. Froofy booze if you change your mind about drinking."

"Sounds nauseating."

Adrienne shrugged and started the car. "You're kind of setting yourself up for an *I want to be miserable* kind of night anyway, might as well let someone else do the cooking."

I didn't have a comeback.

Back at home, I pulled on clothes that would be acceptable in public, wincing at my reflection when I caught the hint of faint green vines and red roses on my breasts and stomach.

At the restaurant, Adrienne, Carly, and Reese kept up the conversation through drink orders—water for me—and the first round of endless chips and salsa.

I was grateful I'd already told Carly about work, so I didn't need to deal with her sympathy for that on top of everything else. She'd insisted she was quitting too, and I made her promise not to. I had a bad experience with one partner, one she rarely had to deal with, and she loved her job.

Carly snapped her fingers in front of my face. "Earth to Daria. You home?"

"I'm sorry, what?" Did they ask me something? I shook my head, trying to clear away the fog.

Adrienne pursed her lips. "Who would win in a fight between Barney the Purple Dinosaur, and the yellow Teletubby."

"Laa-Laa," I corrected her before the rest of my brain caught up. "Wait, what? No you weren't."

Reese snorted. "Because the purple one would kick all their asses. Obviously."

"Barney is purple too," Carly said.

"But Barney is a dinosaur, which means he's extinct, and Teletubbies are English. One still exists one doesn't." Adrienne's logic made more sense than I wanted it to.

"Really, what were we talking about?"

Adrienne sipped her drink. Did she get more reserved when she was drunk instead of less? Be interesting to find out. "How to pull you back to our world."

"She's just dick-stracted." Carly looked pleased with her own joke.

Adrienne looked at her wide-eyed and shook her head. "We're not talking about that."

"About what?" Reese asked. "It's rude to keep secrets in a group like this."

"About the two sexy swim coaches who turned her into a cougar," Carly said.

I sighed. Apparently we were talking about it. "It was just a one-time thing." The words tasted rancid, and I tried to wash them down with water. I should've gotten a drink, but then I'd down it and want another and another.

Carly stared at me. "But you were so happy yesterday morning."

"Two younger men at once, who wouldn't be?" Reese wasn't drinking either. At least I was in good company. I had a hard time getting a read on her; she was flashy and direct and stunning and had an amazing voice, but she rarely talked about herself and frequently seemed like she was holding part of herself back.

"Her kids walked in on them." Adrienne winced and snapped her mouth shut.

Yup. No filter. "It wasn't that bad. But Alana's old enough to know what we'd been up to."

Carly sucked in a sharp breath through her teeth. "Ouch."

"It's fine." I didn't sound the least bit convincing. "One time thing, like I said. As long as Alana forgives me."

Reese huffed and nibbled on a chip.

"You have thoughts?" If we were going to dissect my life at the dinner table, we might as well go all in.

Reese shrugged. "Too many people are willing to give up love for fleeting moments." She sounded like she spoke from experience.

Irritation rankled over me. "This is not love, and my girls are *not* fleeting moments."

"I didn't mean it like that." Reese held up her hands, as if in surrender. "But kids *are* adaptable and what pisses them off today makes them happy tomorrow. Yours already understand what's going on with Adrienne, Dustin, and Phillip. Unless you think their lifestyle is unnatural."

I glared at her. "You're making a lot of assumptions." I looked at Adrienne. "You know I don't have any problems with you at all, don't you? And I don't have an issue with the girls being around it, and I love that they understand it."

"I know." Adrienne nodded. "I also get that introducing new people directly into your home is different. Alana's obviously already attached, and if things go bad… I get it."

At least someone did. "Exactly. Which is why I've ended it. One. Time. Thing." If I said it often enough, I might convince myself. Something occurred to me. I turned to Carly. "You're being awfully quiet."

"Because you don't want to hear it."

Might as well. Everyone else had said their piece. "Try me."

Carly twisted her mouth. "I'm with Reese on this one—the intent not the poor choice of words. Being married to Joe fucked with you. But yesterday? The only time I've ever seen you that happy was when your kids were born. You've never smiled like that when you're talking about a relationship. But I also know you're more in touch with yourself than pretty much anyone. You're so fucking self-aware that it's beauty and pain at the same time. If you're telling yourself this is the right decision, you know you best."

"Thank you." I didn't come across as smugly as I wanted, because I was still trying to convince myself I was making the right decision to dial my relationship back with Colin and Tanner.

It had been less than a day. My body was still riding the high of the levels of attention they gave me. Once I had some time and distance, I'd be able to admit I loved the praise more than the individuals.

And for tonight, I'd take a tipsy Adrienne back to Dustin's, and I'd crash on his couch so I could be there in the morning to start making things up to Alana.

22

tanner

I was surprised and relieved when Colin showed up to swim class on Saturday. He arrived after a few of the students, which didn't leave me time to talk to him in private, but he was all smiles with the kids.

He was exactly the person I knew, and had grown up with...

And had never realized how he felt about me.

The thought slammed into my head, the way it had been over and over since yesterday. It didn't bring any additional insight, so I shoved it aside, the way I had over and over since yesterday.

Class went as smoothly as normal, with one tiny difference. Whenever I asked Colin something directly, or started a conversation with him, his expression would go flat and the little crinkles would vanish from around his eyes.

He always answered, though.

When our time with the students was up, I grabbed his attention. "Can we talk?" I asked.

"About what?" His tone was friendly but cool.

About how I feel about you. But those words stuck in my throat because I didn't know what came after. "About something. Anything."

"I can't. I've gotta run. Maybe next time."

I followed him to the locker room, but instead of changing, he pulled on a T-shirt, grabbed his bag, and headed out in his still-damp trunks.

Maybe he just needed time. I didn't want this gap to exist between us at all, though.

When I pulled my phone from my locker, there was a message waiting for me, from a number I didn't recognize.

"This is Carly," the woman said. "Daria gave me your number, and I'd like to talk. Give me a call back."

Daria. The name sent a flash of hope rushing through me. The feeling didn't erase my stuckness over the Colin situation, but it did give me a glimmer of hope to focus on. Daria had said Carly was her best friend. This had to be promising.

I dialed Carly's number without hesitation. When she answered I said, "This is Tanner Hagen. You left me a message about Daria?"

"Sort of," Carly said. "She asked me to give you a call and talk to you about a building appraisal? I'm hoping we can find a time you can show me this rec center you're looking at."

Oh. Right. "I'm not sure, but I can call the owner and see what his schedule is like. When can I call you back?"

"This is nothing formal. It only needs to be you, so I can tell you if the property is worth pursuing or not. You'll get an official appraisal from your lending bank. If you have keys, let me know when you're free, and you can take me on a walk through."

I didn't want to go back to an empty apartment, and if this was Daria's friend, maybe I could extract a little *how is she* information at the same time. "Is it too much to hope for now?"

"I guess I can catch up on The Bachelor another time." Carly's huff was loud, but her voice was light.

"Are you sure? You're not dying to find out who she chooses?"

Carly clucked. "I'm hoping she picks them all, but given the number of episodes left, that seems unlikely. I can be there in an hour if that works."

"I'll be here." That gave me an hour to kill, and that meant maybe I could lose myself in swimming.

Lap after lap, my mind certainly stayed fixed on a single point, but not my time or form. I was looping on the conversation—or lack thereof—with Colin. When I tried to shove that aside, thoughts of Daria were waiting to take its place.

Three days of screwing around—literally and otherwise—and I was hooked on both of them. But it was more than that. I had something with each of them before this week too. A solid bond, a real friendship, but was it more? The three of us were good together.

Life looked dreary when I tried to imagine a future without either of them in it.

I reached the end of a lap, came up for air, and realized there was a woman standing a few feet back from the pool. When I wiped the water from my eyes, I saw frosted hair, a stunning figure, and her crossed arms.

I climbed from the pool, and I knew without looking that she took the opportunity to look me over while I dried off. I held up a hand to indicate I needed a moment, and when I finished she was still watching me.

And a week ago, as long as she wasn't a student's parent, I would have seized the opportunity to see how deep her appreciation ran. Today, there was no interest. I joined her. "Can I help you?"

"Now I know at least one thing she sees in you." She extended her hand. "Carly. We spoke on the phone."

"Tanner." I shook her hand, but my mind was on her comment. That meant Daria had talked about me in a way that evoked that kind of response. "I appreciate you taking the time to do this."

"I'd do a lot for Daria. This is no big deal though. Do you want to give me the grand tour, and I'll tell you when I need to see more or less?"

I nodded, and gestured. "This is the pool."

She laughed. "Thanks. I might not have figured

that out." Her voice was teasing. "Make sure I don't fall in."

I stepped away long enough to pull on some clothes. It took a few hours to go through the entire building, and I was grateful for the distraction. Carly was good at keeping up a train of small talk, and unfortunately even better at steering the conversation from Daria every time I asked.

Carly wanted to look closer at, and take pictures of things I hadn't put much thought into. Tile and paint and the basement. I was worried she'd home in on the chlorine smell in the classrooms, but she assured me that was an HVAC issue, and it appeared to be fixable.

We were at the far end of the building, in the large gymnasium no one had used in years for anything but stacking chairs, when she proclaimed she was done.

"How serious is it, doc?" I tried to keep my voice light, but braced myself for the news that this place was worth more torn down and rebuilt.

She flipped through her notebook, and thumbed through her phone. "I did some research on this place yesterday. On the existing owner and financing terms, the building's history, and more."

"Okay?"

Carly finally looked at me. "The owner is telling the truth. The place needs some work, and I mean *a lot* of work, but none if it is structural."

"So why…" I thought back to the conversation

with Davenport, who was so insistent that the place was utter shit. "A banker told me not to bother."

"Ah. That's one of the things I found in my research. There's a clause in the existing loan that if the building falls into a certain level of disrepair, the bank can foreclose. My guess is, your guy is desperate to sell, before that happens, so he doesn't lose his equity."

Holy shit. "Son of bitch."

Carly shrugged. "Bankers are bastards."

"So what do I do?" I was trying to keep my hope subdued. This didn't erase my current issues, but it was nice to have a bright spot. As long as she didn't shatter it.

Carly pulled a card from her purse and handed it to me. "Reach out to this guy—he's not as much of a bastard as most, I promise—and tell him you consulted with Daria and she referred you. Show him your proposal, and make an offer on the building that's more than the asking price."

"That's a lot of money."

"The building is worth more. Or it will be once you put your ideas into place. Never fuck someone over on property—Karma's a bitch."

I couldn't help but hope that was true for Davenport. "Thank you. Now will you tell me how Daria is?"

"No. I'm sure you'll see her when she drops Alana off at practice."

I had my doubts. "Just a hint?"

"If she wanted you to know, she'd tell you. I'm sorry. She's made her decision."

Fuck fuck fuck. "At least ask her to call me?"

Carly shook her head. "Do you think she hasn't already considered that? I really am sorry, but I will side with her every time, and this is what she's doing." Carly truly did sound sorry.

Daria wouldn't talk to me. Colin wouldn't talk to me.

I was getting everything I ever thought I wanted, but without them, the joy felt flat.

23
daria

DUSTIN MUST HAVE SAID something to Alana because she was talking to me again. Not a lot of words, but the venom behind them was gone. She almost seemed contemplative.

I let the girls plan our Saturday and Sunday, telling them they had to share the schedule. We shopped, we watched movies, and we went to the batting cages.

Sunday night, Harmony gave me a hug as I was putting her into bed and told me I was the best mom she'd ever had. The sentiment was sweet enough I decided not to ask for her to clarify.

When I walked out of Harmony's room and closed the door behind me, Alana was waiting in the hall.

"Mom? You give up a lot for us, don't you?"

I didn't know where the question came from, but I didn't like the phrasing. "Everything I do for you, I do because I want to."

"But if we weren't here, you'd be doing other things."

What the hell? "What's with the questions?"

Alana grabbed one arm with her other hand. "Have you dated since you and Joe got divorced?"

"Don't call your father by his first name."

"You do. And you're not answering my questions." She finally looked at me.

I tried to be as honest with my girls as possible, but how much of this conversation did I want to have with her? "I've seen people, yes."

"But we've never met any of them," Alana said.

Because fuckbuddies didn't come home with me. Thoughts of Tanner and Colin assaulted me, and I swallowed down any reaction before it could leak into the conversation. "I haven't been close enough with any of them."

"Oh. Do I have to stop going to swimming lessons?"

"No, sweetie. Of course not. Tanner and Colin are qualified teachers, and as long as you enjoy going, you can keep doing so."

"Will you keep talking to them?"

"I assume so. They're good, kind people." It would take some time to move past what happened between us, which was my mistake for letting it mean more—for letting them take up too much space in my heart—but Alana wouldn't pay the price for that.

Alana gave me a hug, which she hadn't done at bedtime in years. "Night, Mom."

"Good night, sweetie." I wasn't sure if the conversation was related to what she said to me on Friday night, or if there was more to it. I was just grateful to have my girl happy with me again.

MONDAY MORNING, I was forced to face the reality that I was unemployed. How had I let myself get so distracted that I let those consequences seem smaller in my mind? I needed to file for benefits, find a lawyer, and sift through the referrals friends were sending me.

I brought my laptop into the living room, so I could hang out with the girls while I did all of the online stuff. Normally I didn't mix work and motherhood, but this was a unique instance.

As I was going through email, my phone rang. I frowned at the name *Kandace* on the screen. It would be so easy to ignore this, but responsibility and the desire to tell them off for what they'd done to me, won out. "This is Daria." I kept my tone cool.

"Hi." Kandace sounded... concerned? "Are you feeling all right this morning? How was the time off?"

Was she fucking kidding me? "I've been better. What can I do for you?"

"I was hoping to see you online this morning, so I'm just calling to make sure you're okay." She sounded serious.

And like she was having a different conversation

that I was. "Besides the fact that Bernie let me go last week, I'm great."

"He *what*?" Kandace's volume spiked.

Apparently he also hadn't told everyone. "He said I was irresponsible for taking the rest of the week off when you told me to, because I'd been working for him."

"No. Nuh-uh," Kandace said. "How the fuck have you not served us with papers yet?"

"It's been a long weekend."

Kandace sighed. "You don't have to respect this request, but I'm asking you to please hold off on legal action. I *will* resolve this, and you'll be back with us soon. If you still want to be."

"I won't make any decisions for a day or so, but I am filing for benefits and putting out feelers."

"That's fair. I'll be in touch soon. I promise," Kandace said. "And I am so sorry."

Sorry didn't make the situation better, but I thanked her like the professional I was, and hung up.

A text came through from Carly less than five minutes later. *Kandace just called me. Begged me not to quit. Is that your doing?*

Sort of. I guess, I sent back. Maybe Kandace was serious. Would I really go back to The Raphael Group if they gave me the chance? Not if I had to work for Bernie anymore. Not if I had to put in ridiculous hours and take last minute business trips and surrender a flexible schedule. It might be hard for me to make those demands anywhere, but I'd find some-place that would let me.

A few minutes after that, my phone rang again. My heart flipped and fell flat when I saw Colin's name on the screen. Now was as good a time as any to start in on the phony *we're just friends* again act, until I believed it. "Grand Central Station."

"No, Mommy. This is the Lane Residence." Harmony didn't look up from her TV show.

Colin laughed. "I'm sorry, I was looking for Daria Lane. I must have the wrong number." Despite his teasing tone, something heavy lay underneath.

I knew what that was like. "Hey. What's up?" As I spoke, I wandered toward the kitchen, and hopefully away from quite so much eavesdropping.

"I have a lawyer's name for you. It took a little longer than I thought for Brooke to track something down," he said.

"Thank you. I'm hoping I won't need it, but send it over."

"Dropping it in an email now."

This was the point where I should thank him again, and hang up. But I liked the sound of his voice. I missed it already. I didn't want to go. "How are you?"

"I'm okay." His voice said he was anything but.

"Obvious lie is obvious." I called him on it before I could think about if I wanted to go down that road. "How are you really?"

"You actually want to know?"

"I actually do." It was true. I cared and I couldn't shut that off.

Colin's sigh echoed in my ear. "Well, I'm incapable of casual sex without an emotional attachment, I've been lying to myself for years about my relationship with my best friend, and I don't know what to do next. Sorry you asked?"

My heart was cracking. Again. But, "No. I'm not. So you and Tanner..."

"There's no *me and Tanner*." Colin's laugh was bitter.

"I'm sorry." I needed those words to encompass so much more than they were capable of.

"It's okay. I made my own decisions, these are the consequences. I'm a big boy."

"Yeah you are." I winced as the teasing slipped out. "I shouldn't have said that." Did I need to monitor everything that came out of my mouth now?

"That's okay, too," Colin said. "I've been holding this inside for so long, it made me resent him. Our relationship means exactly what he said it did. Exactly what you said."

But did it? His words sliced through me. I desperately wanted to say *I was wrong*, and tell him it meant more. *He* meant more. I looked up to find Alana watching from across the room. "I'm sorry," I said again.

"Me too. I'll see Alana at practice?"

I nodded. He couldn't see me. "You will. Talk to

you then." I hung up before either of us could say something I didn't know how to deal with.

I spent the rest of the day bouncing between waiting for Kandace to get back to me, looking for new work, and trying not to act like a lovesick teenager by staring at Colin's email in my inbox

It had a lawyer's name and said *good luck*. It wasn't even as though he'd sent me something worth swooning over. Tanner called me, and I let it go to voicemail. He sent a follow-up text that said *talk to me. Please.*

I wanted to. The simple request left an ache in my chest. Instead, I replied with *let me know if it's an emergency. Otherwise, Alana will see you at practice.*

When my phone buzzed almost immediately after with another text, I wasn't sure if I was happy or irritated with Tanner's persistence. But it was from Kandace, asking me to give her just one more day.

I told her *fine*. Not that my brain would be happy with another day like today. I had to at least start sending resumes out, or I'd go nuts.

Tuesday morning, I woke up to a quiet house. Super quiet. Too quiet. I jolted out of bed with a start, and stalked toward the girls' rooms. Both empty, with their beds made. What the fuck? Whispers drifted up from downstairs and relief trickled in at the familiar voices.

I padded down to the living room to find Alana and Harmony watching Beauty and the Beast with the sound off, and eating cereal. Not completely unheard of, but not normal, either.

"Hi, Mom." Alana seemed completely back to herself. "You don't have to worry about breakfast or dishes. I'm taking care of it."

Maybe not quite herself. I'd ask what she wanted or what she was up to, but I didn't want to ruin the mood. I didn't usually allow them to eat breakfast in front of the TV, but they were behaving.

Alana whispered something to her sister, and Harmony set her bowl on the coffee table and ran up to me.

"Mommy, I want to swim like Alana does."

That was new. Harmony liked to play in the water, but she'd never shown any interest in more. I looked past her to Alana, who wasn't watching us, but who was sitting very still, her head half-turned in our direction.

What was she up to?

"Do you want to compete the way Alana does? Or do you just want lessons?"

Harmony glanced over her shoulder then back at me. "Lessons?"

Alana huffed, set her bowl next to Harmony's, and joined us. "She told me earlier that she wanted Colin to teach her to swim."

Now I knew what Alana was up to, but still wasn't sure why. I crouched so I was eye-level with Harmony. "Do you want that, or did your sister tell you to ask for that?"

"I want that." Harmony nodded. She sounded much more certain this time. Alana was a decent manipulator, but Harmony wasn't a great liar.

"Okay. We'll talk to him this afternoon when we take Alana to practice."

"You could call him now," Alana said.

Was she looking for assurance that she wouldn't have to give up swimming? I still didn't understand. "It's early. This afternoon will be fine."

Harmony cheered and Alana scowled.

I needed coffee before I could dig deeper into her motivations, but I was happy she was talking to me again. Fortunately making coffee took minimal brain power, and within a few minutes, the machine was hissing and steaming and the incredible smell of consciousness was drifting my way.

Coffee in hand, I made myself comfortable at the kitchen table. This was life back to normal. Or, it would be once I was working again. The girls would start school in a few weeks, we'd be back to hectic schedules and meals when we had time.

And making plain, boring, casual-and-completely-friendly-and-nothing-more small talk with my daughter's swim coaches.

When I was done with my first cup of coffee, I worked my way through a semblance of a morning routine on auto-pilot, and settled back in the kitchen. No news from Kandace, not that I expected any overnight. Colin's name still sat in my inbox, teasing me.

It was barely eight when someone rang the front bell.

"I'll get it, so you can keep working," Alana was already on her feet.

Did she know who it was, or was this part of her campaign of helpfulness? "I'll get it." If she'd done something nuts like call Colin or Tanner, what would I say? *Nice to see you, have a nice day*?

I had to.

I opened the door to find Kandace on the other side.

She gave me a warm smile. "I'm sorry to drop by unannounced. I was on my way into the office and I realized I need to have this conversation face to face with you. You deserve that."

"Come on in." I stepped aside, squashing my curiosity under the heavy weight of professionalism and being a good hostess. "Do you want some coffee? Anything else?"

"I'm really trying to cut back on the caffeine, thanks."

"Alana, will you and Harmony go play upstairs for a little while?" I expected a protest with my request.

Instead, Alana grabbed Harmony's hand and led her up to their rooms.

Kandace and I took seats at the table. She let out a short sigh. "I'd love to make small talk, but I think you're anxious to hear what I have to say."

"I am." I hoped it didn't require me to use that lawyer's number from Colin, but we'd see.

She nodded. "I'm sorry it took me so long to get back to you. I had a lot to get through, including some red tape with the other partners, but we pushed things through because of the critical nature of the situation."

It sounded so serious. It was to me, but she had to be talking about more. I didn't dare interrupt.

"We've been having issues with Bernie for a while," Kandace said. "Every one of us was invited to join the firm because we all share some key values that make an organization like this work. It had become clear that he wasn't on the same page as us after all, so we've parted ways with him. You weren't the cause, but your firing was that final straw."

"Oh." That was good news, wasn't it? Not for him, but the asshole fired me, and that wasn't the first run-in I'd had with him.

"Come back to work for us. If you've got other offers, we'll match them."

I stared at Kandace, processing the words, and then the damn in my mind broke. It was a good job. They'd given me a lot of opportunities, I enjoyed the other partners, and working with Carly was awesome.

"I can't go back to the way things were before." The words tumbled out, contrary to my thoughts. My mouth knew me better than my mind sometimes. "The long hours, the last-minute business trips... I don't want it to be five or ten years from now, or even one, and I realize I've missed my girls growing up."

Kandace smiled. "That's more than reasonable. I'll put that in your rehire offer, and if you say you'll come back, you will be paid for last week and any days this week. You've got skills that will be hard to replace, and not just at the resume level. You know our business, you know how to work with our people, and we like your approach to work and your drive."

"Put it all in writing, that I get at least a week's notice for travel and I'm not on call on weekends, and I'll come back."

"Fantastic." Kandace grabbed her phone and made some notes. We agreed I'd start again tomorrow —she offered to give me the rest of the week, but I'd go stir crazy if I took that long—and that she'd get me an updated rehire offer within a few hours.

I sent Kandace on her way and tried to fall into the fantastic news. I didn't have to look for a new job, or sue the old one, or do the math about how long my savings would last.

Which meant I could save the lawyer information from Colin for a different rainy day.

As his name passed through my head, the gnawing that had been inside for days was back. The pit that missed them both far more than was reasonable.

It had only been a few days. I'd get over this feeling. There wasn't another choice, because I had two wonderful lives, two children, who needed at least one parent that cared. Me dating Colin and Tanner would detract from that. As Alana put it, that would hurt her as well as me when things didn't work out.

And I couldn't walk into any relationship knowing that.

24
colin

I KNELT NEXT to the motorcycle in Brooke's garage—her much cleaner than a few days ago garage—and examined the primer on the gas tank. The base coat was dry, set, and sanded. It was the perfect canvas.

Last time I said that, it was looking over Daria's gorgeous frame. I missed her terribly.

Paige, my niece, had rebuilt this bike. It had been her dad's before he passed away when she was a kid, and she was determined to give it a good life.

She hadn't quite figured out the right look for it, this would be the third time I'd painted the thing, but I didn't mind. She made the bike purr, and I'd help her make it look good.

Her twin brother, Bryan, was just as brilliant, but in an academic direction. They were seventeen, and in a few weeks would head into their last year of high school.

Brooke would never admit it out loud, but she was already wondering how she was going to cope when they went off to college. Like Daria, she'd given everything to her kids, and doubled down when they lost their father.

The twins were at track and field practice, with Paige cheering on Bryan as he and the team prepped for early school year matches. I'd already cleared the garage, the attic, and taken most of the large trash to the dump. I wanted to tackle the creaky old barn on the back of Brooke's property, but she'd reiterated it was off limits, so I was prepping Paige's bike for painting. Was I doing anything I could to not think about Tanner and Daria? Damn right.

I glanced over my shoulder at the sound of the door from the house to the garage opening. Brooke stepped into the garage, and I gave her a nod and went back to work.

"Who's Daria?" Brooke's soft question tied my insides in knots.

"Where did that come from?"

Brooke shrugged. "Sisterly instinct."

Bullshit. "You already know who she is. She's a mom of one of the kids in our classes."

"And a friend?"

"Of course." *Just a friend.* Tanner's voice taunted me in my head.

"A good enough friend she let the two of you stay at her house, while no one else was going to be there."

I stopped what I was doing and turned to Brooke. "You have a point?"

"Just being nosey."

"Without question." I wanted to get back to work, but there was no way I'd have the focus now. So much for ignoring my problems.

Brooke crossed her arms and leaned against the doorframe. "It's just that you're here moping over Tanner, but you've got some lady friend…"

"Daria's not some throwaway rebound fuck." I winced as the words passed my lips. That wasn't what Brooke said.

She looked surprised as well. "Not all of us think in terms of flings and hook-ups." She almost sounded hurt.

She hadn't dated much since she lost her husband. And not really before that, either. We were raised in a religious household, and my sisters were all taught their biggest goal in life was to find a man and make him happy.

Brooke took longer to lose her faith than I did, and even though she was older, there were still some things she wasn't comfortable with. I'd never delved into whether or not one of them was casual sex, but I assumed.

I sighed. "Daria… The thing is… It's complicated."

"More complicated than you loving Tanner for years and not telling him?"

"So much more complicated. What's with the twenty-questions?"

Brooke pushed away from the house and joined me. She settled on an upside-down milk crate we had out here to use as a stool. "I worry about you. I'm not complaining about the fact that you've eaten through my *I'll never do* list, but it does make a woman curious."

How was I supposed to explain this to her when there were parts of it I couldn't make sense of myself. "I think I'm falling for both of them." The words tumbled out unfiltered. "Not in a love triangle kind of way, but in an *I want them both long term* kind of way."

"Still sounds like a love triangle…"

"No. Because I don't want to pick."

She twisted her mouth. "You have to, don't you?"

"I don't know. I don't think so." God, I hoped not. Though at this point, neither Tanner nor Daria was a choice, so it didn't matter.

Brooke furrowed her brow. "So, like… polygamy?"

"No. More like marriage, but with three people." Oh, shit. Did I just say marriage? Nope. The three of us didn't have that. Nope.

Why couldn't we have that? After a bit more getting to know each other. But…

"Is that a thing?" Brooke asked.

"Legally? Probably not. Emotionally… Yes."

She shook her head. "I don't know how that's possible, but I can tell you're miserable, and you're the reason I understand that someone doesn't have to pick between liking men and women. Of course, I didn't think it was so literal."

I let out a strained laugh. "It's usually not."

"Can I meet her?"

"Things aren't happening that way." This was reality, no matter how much I wanted otherwise. It didn't matter if Daria felt the same, even. She had her reasons for putting an end to that side of our relationship. "She's choosing to focus on her kids."

"Ah. That I understand. You know, you'll have to talk to Tanner eventually. Either cut him off altogether, or make things right."

One of those options made my gut churn and the other didn't seem possible. "I talk to him at practice."

"That's not what I mean."

"I know."

Brooke stood and patted me on the shoulder. "If anyone can figure this out, it's you."

"Thanks." I wished I could agree with her.

I worked on my sketch a little longer, penciling something out for Paige to take a look at when she got home, then headed to swim class. I arrived just as the first students were showing up, so I could give them my attention instead of talking to Tanner.

He gave me a tentative smile and a wave, and I nodded back.

When Alana showed up, Daria and Harmony were with her. Daria's smile was pasted on, but she looked good. Why couldn't she and Tanner and I go talk somewhere and make this work between the three of us?

Would either of them want that, even if me being with them was an option? Sharing for fun was one thing, but I was being delusional even hoping for that kind of long-term attention from one of them.

Daria approached me. "Colin, hey. Harmony wants to start taking swim lessons."

"Sure. We can get her signed up." Would this be us long term? No fun. No banter. Not even a little bit of *how are you today*?

I got Harmony registered for classes, Daria sent the girls off to get changed, and she settled into the bleachers to watch.

This was going to suck.

We kicked off class before Tanner could draw me into another round of *let's talk, but I don't know about what*.

Things ran smoothly. The older kids practiced with Tanner and I worked with the younger ones. The longer the afternoon went on, the rowdier and more impatient the younger kids grew, which was standard, until I decided it was time to call it a day for them. "All right, everyone out of the water."

I was focused on making sure every kid was out, when a series of laughs and shouts caught my attention. Two of the kids were splashing water at each other as I raised myself from the pool. "Come on, guys. Pool safety," I called.

"Can't cath me," Edward shouted, and ran from another of the boys.

Shit. "Hey, no running," I shouted, and moved to chase them. My foot hit the tile at the wrong angle, and I lost my traction. I swore my world slowed to a crawl as my legs slipped from underneath me and the edge of the pool rushed up to meet my face. I couldn't stop myself from—

25

tanner

THE HAPPY SCREAMS of kids were background noise, since I was working with my own students, but Colin's shout drew my attention. I hated that he was only saying the bare minimum to me. That Daria was the same—

I swore my heart stopped when Colin's footing slipped. He was falling at the wrong angle, toward the edge of the pool, and I was on my feet.

His head struck the edge, and I was sprinting.

He didn't surface again, and I was diving into the water.

When I hit the water, my angle wasn't right either. I felt the familiar, excruciating tear in my shoulder, but that didn't matter. Kicked straight for Colin, who wasn't moving, wrapped my good arm around his waist, and hauled him to the surface.

I was vaguely aware of shouting—Daria—telling one of the older boys to help me, and everyone else to get out of the water. She was barking orders at other parents, at everyone.

The only thing I cared about right now was that Colin hadn't opened his eyes.

I lay him on his side on the ground, and he coughed as his eyelids fluttered. Adrenaline had my heart and body running on overdrive, but I couldn't do anything except lay him on his side and make sure he kept breathing.

"There's an ambulance on its way. What do you need?" Daria knelt next to me.

To keep him breathing and conscious. Not lying down but not upright. "Something to prop him up."

"Who? What happened?" Colin tried to sit up.

Daria slid a pool toy behind his head, and I gently nudged him back to lay on it.

"You hit your head," I said.

Colin leaned his weight back. "Oh."

"How's your shoulder?" Daria asked.

Right. The agony screaming through half my torso. I'd most likely torn the rotator cuff again. "It'll be fine." I'd never compete again—the Olympics were definitely out—and it didn't matter, as long as Colin was all right.

"You look worried." Was that a slur to Colin's words? "What happened?"

"You hit your head," I repeated.

He frowned. "Oh."

Double fuck. I'd seen this a few times with other

athletes. I held a finger in front of Colin's face, about two feet away. "Follow the movement, eyes only."

"It's all blurry." Colin stared at my hand and blinked a few times. "Nope. Still blurry."

So this was probably a concussion.

"You take care of him, I'll make sure everyone gets home safely and the place locked up," Daria said.

"Why?" Colin asked. "What happened? Why does my head hurt?"

It was going to be a long night. It didn't matter, as long as he came through this okay. I gave Daria all of the information she needed, and she returned from our lockers a short while later with phones and clothes. I answered Colin's questions as many times as he asked them.

When the ambulance arrived, I told them everything that happened and what I'd done so far, while they strapped Colin to a stretcher.

Daria grabbed my arm before I could follow them outside. "Call me as soon as you know more, please?"

"Sure. Of course." I turned away before I finished the promise, and joined the EMTs and Colin outside. They tried to tell me I needed to meet them at the hospital. Fuck that. "I'm his partner."

I braced myself for Colin to contradict me, but he didn't seem to be paying attention.

The EMT shrugged and pointed me to the passenger seat. I'd take it. The trip took the longest fifteen minutes of my entire life. Would Colin be okay? What if his injuries had been worse? What if I'd never gotten the chance to tell him—

I drew in a shaky breath. That wasn't the case here, but it might have been. I was almost willing to let him walk out of my life because I was too much of a coward to admit I loved him. That I was *in* love with him.

At the hospital, I explained again what happened, and they wheeled Colin away for examination. Filling out paperwork and giving them his information kept me distracted for a little, but not nearly long enough. They showed me to a small room to wait, while he went through X-Ray, MRI, and whatever else they deemed necessary.

I wanted to call Daria, but I didn't have much of an update for her. I sent her a quick text instead. *At the hospital. No more news.*

When she replied with *thanks for letting me know* I felt the tension in the brief message. As soon as he could remember that I'd said it, I was telling him how I felt. That I was wrong and an idiot for not seeing it sooner.

Fuck it, I'd tell him the moment I could talk to him again, and over and over, until he did remember.

A nurse came into the room to give me an update, and paused, staring at me. "You're favoring your arm."

"I have an old injury—torn rotator cuff—I think I re-damaged it." I wasn't worried about that. The pain stayed at a dull roar if I didn't move my shoulder.

"Come on. Let's get you checked out."

"I can't. I'm waiting."

He raised his eyebrows. "Your partner is going to be a while, but I promise to have someone come find you if he's done before you are."

After an examination and a few tests, they confirmed what I already knew—my arm was shot. They gave me a sling, but my injury wasn't the same kind of emergency as Colin's, so my scans would wait.

And then I was back to doing the same.

It was almost ten at night when Colin's doctor found me. "Colin is fine. He has a concussion, but the damage isn't severe. The short-term memory loss is already mostly gone, but expect to still see it occasionally. We do want to keep him overnight for observation, and when he checks out, someone will need to stay with him for at least 24 hours."

"That'll be me. Where is he?"

"I'll have an orderly bring you to his room, and a nurse will be by in a little bit with information about what to do after he checks out."

"Thank you."

I called Brooke, who went from sounding annoyed to hear from me, to definitely irritated that I hadn't let her know sooner, to relieved that Colin was okay.

"Tanner." The edge in her voice stopped me as we were ending the call.

"Hmm?"

"Don't hurt him, or I will hunt you down."

Because of course Colin had told her why he was staying with her. I doubted he used the words *clueless asshat*, but the meaning probably came across that way. "I promise that's the last thing I want."

I called Daria next, and she picked up immediately. "Hey. How is he?" she asked.

"He's all right." It was such a relief to say that. "Concussion, they're keeping him overnight, but he'll be okay."

"Good. How are you? You hurt yourself."

"I'm okay too. Thank you, for taking care of everything at the pool." I'd been aching to talk to her for more than a week, and this was the only conversation that mattered now. I still wanted to tell her I felt like that week at her house was more. That I wanted more from her.

But I understood why she'd stepped back, and Colin was who mattered tonight. And every night. Every day. Why did I have to wait until things were desperate to realize how I felt?

Daria had said something.

"I'm sorry. I didn't catch that."

She huffed out a weak laugh. "I asked if you need a ride to your car."

"No, but thank you. I'm staying here for a while."

"Okay. Call me if you need anything." She sounded sincere, and I knew she meant it rather than throwing the words out as a platitude.

"Thank you."

With the phone calls done, I gathered up our bags,

and waited an excruciating 15 more minutes until they finally brought me to Colin.

He was in a regular hospital room, his bed raised enough to have him half sitting. He looked pale, and a frown whispered across his face when he saw me.

Where was I supposed to start? "I'm so—"

"Your arm."

I— what?

"What happened?" Colin asked.

I stared at him. "You're lying there with a dented brain and you're worried about my arm?"

He shrugged.

A hysteria-tinged laugh slipped past my lips. "Are you kidding me right now? I was an absolute ass to you. We've barely spoken in days. You could've fucking drowned, and you want to know how my arm is?"

"Well, yeah. It's in a sling. How badly are you hurt?"

"God damn it, Colin. I swear I don't deserve you." I stopped next to his bed.

One corner of his mouth tugged up. "You really don't. Why did you tell them you were my partner?"

He remembered that. Of all the things… "Wishful thinking."

And now Colin's frown was back.

I had to make this right. "I'm sorry for being dim. For not recognizing how you felt about me. For not admitting how I feel about you. I don't know if it's too late, but I love you Colin. I'm lost without you."

"I should hit my head more often. The hallucinations are amazing."

"I just poured my heart out to you."

"I wouldn't call it a pour. How's it feel, by the way? To confess your heart's desire and not get the response you hoped for?"

I worked my jaw.

Colin grinned. "I love you too. I didn't stop feeling a lifetime of adoration in the last few days."

I laughed. "All right. I deserved that."

"I get a kiss, right? *I love you* comes with kisses?" Colin asked.

It absolutely did. I pressed my lips softly to his, not wanting to hurt him, but I lingered, not wanting to pull away. How was this so perfect? And how did I almost walk away from it?

26
colin

I WANTED to drag out the teasing a little longer, and make Tanner sweat, but I was also so giddy to hear him say those words. And if I thought the kisses were good before, when we were *just fooling around* — as if— this tender, concerned Tanner and the way his lips moved against mine, lit my soul on fire.

"Come back home when they discharge you?" Tanner murmured against my mouth.

I smiled and kissed him again. "Okay. But only because you're pretty when you're worried about me."

"I'm pretty all the time," Tanner said.

I wanted to keep kissing, and maybe more, but the increasingly insistent beeps from my blood pressure monitor said that might not be a good idea.

Tanner pulled back, looking as reluctant as I felt, seconds before a nurse walked into the room.

She looked between the two of us, then took a look

at the machine. "This is going to set off an alarm every time one of your numbers goes out of whack." The warning in her voice was clear.

Heat flooded my cheeks. "I'll keep that in mind."

She left us alone, and Tanner settled on the edge of the bed instead. "I guess the hand job has to wait until they release you," he teased.

I grinned. "Probably a good idea. Both parts of it." The monitor beeped loudly again, and I forced myself to calm down.

Tanner's laugh didn't help. But it did sound wonderful. I'd missed him.

"Are you going to tell me what's wrong with your arm?" I asked.

He looked down at the sling and a frown whispered across his face before vanishing again. "I tore my rotator cuff."

"What?" My gut sank. "How?"

"It doesn't matter."

"Pulling me out of the pool. Oh, fuck. The Olympic trial."

He shook his head. "It doesn't matter. I'd make the same choice every single time if I had to."

"But you pushed so hard. You—"

Tanner rested his palm on my cheek. "It doesn't matter. You being safe matters." His sincerity was heavy.

"I still feel bad."

"Because you're you." Tanner smiled. "Another

thing I love you for—you care about people. It's never just lip service."

Another thing I love you for. Hearing that wasn't getting old anytime soon. Or ever.

"I'm going to say this, not because it makes a difference in how I feel about the situation, but in case it helps you," Tanner said. "I barely squeaked out that qualifying time. What was I going to do? Spend money we've been saving for years to fly to tryouts? I wasn't coming home with the gold—or the bronze— no matter how much I wanted to believe otherwise."

"You might have." If anyone could do it, Tanner could. He made so many things happen that I was pretty sure were by pure force of will.

"It doesn't matter. You being all right matters. I'll say that as many times as I have to for you to know I mean it." He kissed my fingertips. "Get some rest, so I can take you home."

That wasn't happening. Not with Tanner's *I love yous* floating in my thoughts and heart. Instead, we caught up. He told me about the building estimate, which was incredible news, and a far more interesting story than mine about cleaning out Brooke's garage.

"That is, if you still want to work with me," Tanner said.

I looked at him with disbelief. "Partner in every sense of the word. You can't shuffle me off just because I hurt my brain. Of course I still want to do this." We'd have to figure out the logistics of the fact that neither of us would be teaching swimming for a little while, and get bank approval if we wanted the building, but now seemed like as good a time as any to start expanding our operations.

We talked a little longer, but sleep stole in without my permission. I woke up to sunlight striking my window, and Tanner nowhere to be found. I grabbed the nurse, asked about discharge, and if she'd seen where he went.

She told me she'd find the doctor for the first, but that Tanner wasn't here when she clocked in half an hour ago.

My heart sank. I shouldn't have expected him to spend the night here, that was ridiculous. But his being gone was enough to make me wonder if I remembered last night right.

The doctor stopped by to do one more check-up, gave me the final information I needed to check out, and told me I could be on my way as soon as I had a ride. I should probably call Tanner or Brooke.

I was mostly dressed, pulling on my socks, when someone knocked. "You decent?" Tanner called.

His voice made my heart flutter, in spite of my doubt. "Yup."

He walked in with Brooke, who smiled when she saw me, and gave me a tight hug. "So glad you're all right. This dummy didn't tell me you were even hurt until nearly ten last night."

Tanner shrugged. "I was too busy worrying about you, Colin. Speaking of, sorry I wasn't here when you woke up. I called her to take me to my car, and explain what happened. I thought we'd be back before you were ready to go."

"Last night happened, right? All of it?" I needed to know that now, and I didn't care who heard.

Tanner crossed the room, cradled my face with his good hand, and brushed his lips over mine, as if it were the most natural thing in the world.

Brooke gasped.

"If you mean the pink elephants, no. Those weren't real." Tanner kissed me again. "But this is. The part where I told you I love you is very, very, real."

"It's about freaking time," Brooke said.

I laughed in spite of myself, and kissed Tanner back. It felt right to clench his shirt in my fists and press my body to his, and with no alarms to say my blood pressure was too high, I could keep tasting him. Feeling him. All of it.

My cock twitched and hardened, and I let go. I wasn't comfortable doing *all* of this in front of my sister.

"I'll go move your stuff from my car to Tanner's," Brooke said. "Keys."

Tanner fished his keys out, never pulling away from me, and handed them over.

As soon as she was gone, he and I broke out in embarrassed laughter. This was so right.

A nagging in the back of my mind said something was missing. Someone. I could think about Daria later —for now, I was going to enjoy finally having Tanner.

27
daria

WAITING for news from Tanner was agonizing. I didn't care that it was late when he finally called, it only mattered that he and Colin were both all right.

They were friends, of course I was worried. If something happened to Carly, I'd be worried too.

This felt different though. Because I was making my worry for Tanner and Colin more, or because it actually was more? And did my feelings matter any more than they had this morning, if seeing the men was bad for my girls?

Nope.

My sleep was restless and my mind filled with questions about what I wanted versus what I should be doing.

In the morning, I dragged myself through coffee. Kandace's rehire offer was exactly what she promised, and I was going back to work today. I needed something to occupy my mind.

Allyson Lindt

Harmony wanted cereal for breakfast, and Alana said she'd do the same. That made things easy. Alana even filled both their bowls again—the help was nice, but what was she up to?

"Mommy, can I play the games on the back of the box?" Harmony asked.

At least that was normal. "Eat your food first."

"Okay." She shoveled a spoonful into her mouth. "Artnclmfph mpbuledy?"

I sighed internally, but I was also grateful to see my little one acting like herself. "Swallow before you talk." I told Harmony.

She did as requested. "Are Colin and Tanner going to be our new daddies?"

I choked on my coffee. This was why I never brought men into the house. But they were different. And the girls had liked them before I ever slept with Colin and Tanner.

Fuck. This was messy. "Daddy is your daddy." Nonsensical-but-obvious mom statement for the win.

"But Edward has two daddies and two mommies." Harmony ate more of her food.

Alana was strangely quiet for all of this. Where was the *you're so stupid,* followed by *I'm not stupid, you're stupid*?

"Edward's parents divorced then married other people," I said.

Harmony nodded. "And you and Daddy are divorced."

Alana huffed.

208

There it was.

She sank in her seat and crossed her arms.

Or not.

"When I grow up, I'm going to marry Edward and Joanie." Harmony moved on to the next tangent.

Thankfully, this was a conversation I could handle. Well, maybe not, but it was preferable to the previous one. "You can't marry people unless everyone agrees."

"I already asked them," Harmony said. "They said okay."

Because of course my forward-looking child was already planning her wedding. "You'll have to make sure again when we get closer to you being older."

"When will that be?" Harmony asked.

"Ten years." That felt like a safe answer.

Harmony nodded and returned to her cereal.

Thank fuck she'd moved on from the Tanner and Colin question. I'd love it if I could do the same.

The thought gnawed at me. How long until I *could* move on? Because as much as I knew I should, I didn't want to.

Alana finished her breakfast first, walked her bowl to the sink, and rinsed it out before returning to the table. "Mom, it's okay if they are."

I could ask what she was talking about, but the pit in my gut had a pretty good idea. Harmony hadn't asked about Colin and Tanner on her own—she'd had prompting from her older sister.

"They're really nice," Alana said. "And I bet

they'd never cancel a vacation early or make you change your plans last minute, and they're old like you."

Should I be grateful I was just *old* and not *old and gross* like Uncle Dustin? "Colin and Tanner aren't old."

Alana shrugged.

I expected a lot of things out of motherhood, but nothing anywhere had prepared me for this conversation. Part of me had thought I could avoid even introducing one man into their life until they were older, but two? "I'm not getting remarried. Not to them or anything."

There was that nagging pain in my chest again. That murmur of *but I don't want to lose them.*

"Okay." Alana took Harmony's bowl when it was empty, and cleaned those dishes up too, before returning to her chair at the table.

She never dropped a subject unless she thought she was being clever and had a plan. What was she up to?

Harmony pulled the cereal box closer. As she followed the maze on the back with her finger, she told a story about the pony who lived in the forest at the end. This was a continuation of the same story she'd told last week, while she connected the dots on another picture.

"Mom, can I have an end of summer party?" Alana asked.

Was this what she'd been leading up to? It'd be a

lot of work, but I could enlist help, and it was so much better than talking about how much Tanner and Colin would be in our futures. "Sure."

"Boys and girls?"

I wasn't ready to deal with that. "Some of the parents won't like that, and it will mean fewer people will come."

"Okay. Just girls then."

That was too easy.

"Can it be a pool party?"

Part of my mind was putting together the pieces of Alana's plan, but I couldn't grasp the final goal. "We don't have a pool." I shouldn't have to remind her of that, but my brain was working overtime to guess her next question. "And the rec center isn't good for parties."

"Uncle Dustin has a pool."

Harmony had stopped telling her story and was watching us.

"No. Phillip has a pool." I knew that Dustin and Adrienne spent a lot of time there, but they didn't live at Phillip's. Yet.

Alana looked at me with what she probably assumed were big puppy dog eyes. "Please? I promise not to fight with Harmony for an entire month."

Like that was going to happen. "That should be your goal anyway."

"Pleeeeaaasssse?"

"Please. Please. Please. Please." Harmony joined in.

There were far worse things Alana could ask for, and I still had some of that mom guilt going on. "I'll call Phillip, but if he says *no*, that's that."

"Now?" Alana asked.

"He's working now."

My response earned me another chorus of *pleases*.

I settled for sending him a text instead. If he took a while to reply, I could set the girls up for the morning and start work.

He answered within a few minutes. *Of course. Any weekend, just give me a few days' notice.*

Easy enough. *Thank you.* I replied. *Tell Dustin and Adrienne hi.*

I looked up from my phone to find Alana watching me.

"He says yes, just pick a date."

Alana clapped. "I want it this Saturday. Can I have a new swimsuit? Never mind, it's okay. I'm good with the suit I have. I'm going to go make a list of who to invite." She pushed back from the table and made it up two stairs before she stopped and turned to me again. "Can Tanner and Colin come?"

My heart twisted in on itself. On the one hand, it made sense she'd want her swim coaches at her pool party. On the other hand, my daughter had more convoluted schemes than a daytime soap opera. "I don't know if either of them will be up for swimming by then, and you said girls only."

"But they're your friends not mine. Besides, it never hurts to have more adults watching over things. *Please*."

"Stop." I didn't need another round of Harmony joining in on the begging. "Sit down at the table, Alana." I looked at Harmony. "Hon, would you like to go tell the pony's story to Dumbo?"

Harmony shook her head. "Alana said I could listen when you talked about our new daddies."

Ah, hell. "What are you up to, Alana?" I could assume, but that could be dangerous when it came to her scheming.

"I want a pool party."

I stared at her, hoping she'd fess up without too much prodding. I wasn't up for dragging the truth out of her.

Alana ducked her head. "You've been really sad since they went home. Like *really* sad. And you looked even sadder when you saw them yesterday, and I don't want you to be sad."

"It's been a long few days."

"But I've never seen you so sad. Even when Dad left you weren't sad. You just didn't yell as much anymore."

Guilt, thy name is Mother. I mentally scrubbed my face and tried to find an answer.

"If you want to marry them, that's okay with us," Alana said.

Damn it. Fuck. God fucking damn it. "I don't have

a *let's get married* kind of relationship with Tanner and Colin."

"Yet." Alana's reply echoed the thought I didn't dare indulge. "But how will you know if you could, if you stop talking to them?"

Could someone please stop my children from growing up so quickly? "What happened to *when people break up, other people get hurt*?"

Alana frowned. "But you're already hurt."

"All right." That wasn't what I should say, but my mouth refused to grasp any other words. "I'll invite them to your party, but don't be surprised if they can't make it."

"*Yay.*" Alana and Harmony cheered and clapped in unison.

What was I doing?

I didn't know anymore.

28
tanner

WHEN COLIN and I got home from the hospital, I tugged him into my room. "I'm supposed to keep an eye on you for at least twenty-four hours. Doctor's orders."

"We don't want to go against the doctor." Colin's smile was warm. Genuine. Reassuring.

"My point exactly." I pulled him into bed and pressed myself into his back. This felt natural—how did I miss that before? How did I deny it for so long?

He snuggled closer. "You have no idea how many times I dreamed of something like this."

It was still strange hearing that he'd seen me as more than a friend for so long, but unlike before, my hesitation was gone. I needed to make the most of it. "I'm sorry I didn't see it. In you and in me."

"Did Tanner Hagen just apologize for something?" Colin looked over his shoulder, teasing in his voice.

I laughed. "Don't get used to it."

"Oh, I plan to."

I didn't mean to fall asleep, but the tension and uncertainty that had haunted me for days was lifting, and laying here with Colin felt *so* right.

I woke up to him stirring. The clock said it was nearly noon. I reluctantly extracted myself from the bed, a to-do list ticking off in my head. Still, I had to stop and look at Colin, half awake and looking every bit like my future.

"What?" Colin asked.

I shook my head. "Just basking in the moment."

"Fuck. Give a guy a little love and all the sudden you turn all sappy on me."

I raised an eyebrow. "Are you complaining?"

Colin grinned. "Not even for a second. Are you worried enough to give me a sponge bath?"

"I will make sure you don't get dizzy in the shower." I rolled to straddle his waist, propping myself up on one elbow and searching his face. How did it take me so long to admit I wanted this? Wanted him? How did I almost throw this away?

He tilted his head up to brush his lips over mine, then flopped back, hesitation flitting in his eyes.

"What's wrong?" I asked.

"Just making sure this is real."

Because for me it was new, and for him it was years of waiting, finally realized. "It is. I promise."

Colin used his full body to push me back, the heat

of his chest against mine searing me. His smile was easy and familiar, but I was seeing it differently now. "Good." He kissed me again. "Though I'm not sure I trust you to catch me if I fall, with that bum arm."

"Asshole. Don't fall, then."

"Setting aside the fact that completely contradicts the *getting dizzy* sentiment… Too late." He hopped to his feet. "Shower?"

The tiny stall in his bathroom wasn't made for two people. The tub in mine was barely better, but standing up, we made it work. Except, standing naked as I faced Colin, hot water streaming over us, hesitation and uncertainty seized me in a way I wasn't familiar with.

Not that I wanted to leave. But I didn't know what to do next, with another guy's dick, hard and pressing into my bare hip.

Colin reached past me, pressing flesh to flesh, and grabbed the body wash. "It's a shower. There's no pressure."

He squirted soap into my hand, and then his own, before setting the bottle down again. It didn't matter that he focused on not erogenous regions—my chest, my arms—the way he glided slick palms over my skin was incredible.

I returned the favor as best I could with one arm, memorizing the terrain of his body. I'd seen him almost every day since we were teenagers, frequently with both of us wearing next to nothing, and in even less in the showers at the pool. This was different. Electrifying. I wanted to imprint it in my mind forever.

This specific experience was new, but I had a good idea what I'd want if I were in Colin's place. What I wanted now. I dropped my hand to Colin's cock, and the sound that rumbled from his chest rolled over and through me when I started to stroke.

The angle wasn't the same as if I were doing this for myself, but I'd been jerking off for a long time and it was easy to see if Colin liked what I did.

When he returned the favor, I let out a long groan, and jerked against his tight, slippery grip. He tugged me closer and crushed his mouth to mine. We matched each other stroke for stroke.

Desire and pleasure mounted inside me, wrapping me in the sensations. My need surged toward a bursting point, and my balls tightened. I squeezed Colin harder. Pumped faster. I was barely aware of where his grunts—his body—ended and mine began.

Everything about this was new and amazing, despite the gestures being familiar. This wasn't just physical, there was an emotional connection that ran between us and tied us together. That intensified every sensation and sound and the taste of Colin's kisses and the way he looked with his eyelids fluttering. Hell, even the faint scent of chlorine mixed with soap, as both rinsed down the drain, was arousing.

Colin jerked against my touch with shudders that

matched mine. Orgasm flooded me, and his touch eased up as mine did. I rested my head against his shoulder, and he leaned his weight into my good arm, as we both panted to catch our breath. Water spilled around us, rinsing away the results of our mutual masturbation. I tilted against the wall, letting the cool tile soothe my heated skin.

"God, I love you." Colin's murmur blended with the sound of the shower.

It'd be easy to joke that a good orgasm made a lot of people say that, but I didn't want to lose this moment. I didn't want to play down the warmth bursting in my heart. "I love you too."

I'd had plenty of practice doing things one-handed the first time I tore my rotator cuff, but there was no way I was going to stop Colin from helping me wash my hair, or rinse me clean, or dry me off.

We both got dressed, and wandered into the kitchen for lunch. We'd done this so many times in the past, but today, it was brand new.

"What do you want?" I asked.

Colin shrugged. "Grilled cheese?"

My heart stalled and my step faltered and images of Daria flashed in my mind.

"Are you okay?" Colin asked.

My love life wasn't quite as neatly tied up as I wanted, and I didn't know how to explain the hesitation to Colin. How was I supposed to tell her *I mean it when I say I love you, but there's someone else, too.*

"You miss her," Colin said. "I do too."

There should be a shock of jealousy. Instead, I was relieved to hear he felt the same way. "Yeah." I sighed and tucked the thought away. I didn't want to, but other things needed to happen first. "Grilled cheese it is."

I made food. As we ate, we discussed what came next for the school. We usually slowed classes down significantly during the fall and winter months, and we'd already had a plan to stop teaching completely if I qualified for the Olympics.

The reminder sent a spike of pain through my shoulder, and I shrugged it off with little thought. This was better. I knew this was better. A glance at Colin, and I had no doubt.

We grabbed our phones, to start making phone calls and class cancellations. When I unlocked mine, several missed calls stared back. "Oops."

"Who?" Colin asked.

"John. A bank contact Daria referred me to." I swallowed. "Daria."

"Call her back." Colin's insistence matched the voice in my head.

I was already dialing on speaker phone so Colin could hear.

"Hey." Daria's greeting was a combination of hesitant and hopeful.

Or I wanted it to be. I was pretty sure it was. "Hey. I saw you called."

"Hello," Colin chimed in.

Daria laughed lightly. "How are you both feeling?"

"Like a million, bazillion bucks." Colin answered.

I shook my head. "Not quite, but close."

"Good. I was worried…" The way she trailed off, I expected more. But then several seconds passed.

Was she waiting on one of us? I opened my mouth,

"Alana is having a pool party," Daria said suddenly. "Her not-quite-uncle has a pool and she's inviting her friends and she wants her swim coaches there."

I was surprised, after the fuss Alana put up when she almost walked in on us. Then again, yesterday she was back to her normal, competitive self.

"Neither one of us will be swimming for a while." Colin zoomed in on the obvious.

"I told her that. She said you could sit at the side of the pool with me."

"*She* said that?" I was a teensy bit disappointed that hadn't been Daria's suggestion, but she'd passed the word along, so that was a start.

Daria's huff was light. "I say that too. I'd like to see you both again."

I exchanged looks with Colin and saw my hope reflected back at me. He gave a slight nod.

"We'll be there," I said.

"Good. We'll see you then." Daria gave us the party details then hung up.

I had other calls to return, but I didn't think this conversation could wait.

"How I feel about her doesn't make me love you any less." Colin blurted out before I could figure out how to start the conversation.

"How do you feel about her?" I could use his answer to decipher my own thoughts. But I already know. "Because I'm falling for her—have fallen?—one is only a few steps from the other. But I love you so much."

Colin's smile was now one of my favorite sights. "So maybe we tell her this, instead of holding onto it for years and hoping it becomes something."

"How many years?" I shouldn't ask, but I needed to know how long I'd been an idiot for.

"Fifteen. Fifteen million. Does it matter now that you and I have moved to the next step?"

"When did you get so wise?"

Colin grinned. "I've always been wise, you're just too dense to see it."

I threw a wadded-up napkin at him. "Truth hurts, man. But I hear Daria's brother has both a boyfriend and a girlfriend. That means some people know how to make it work."

"What if we're not two of them?" Colin's hesitation seemed to come out of nowhere.

I shrugged. "Would you rather let the thought gnaw at you and never know one way or the other?"

He shook his head. "No. Definitely not. As long as

I'm not giving you up to have her, then let's see what happens next."

"You're not." I stood and leaned in to kiss him. A gesture that already felt natural, but also new and incredible. "You and me together no matter what. And with any luck, Daria and her kids are a part of that too."

29
colin

THE CALL TANNER received from John was a plea for us to not sue him for the accident. Neither injury happened due to his negligence or the building's disrepair, but Tanner did ask him to help make sure his insurance processed our claims.

The call from Daria's contact at the bank wanted to set an appointment. Tanner and I met with him the next day, and while the conversation seemed to go well, his answer was *I'll be in touch*.

The rest of the week was an odd blur of acquainting myself with Tanner in all new ways, and not knowing what to do with ourselves, thanks to the unplanned vacation. Aside from the occasional headache, I was good within a day or so, but working around his injuries was fun.

I was happy to ride him, blow him, and tease him with two working hands, and he was sexy-sweet trying to figure out how to reciprocate with only one.

This was what I'd wanted just a few weeks ago, and now that I had it, it was so much better than I'd imagined.

Saturday afternoon we headed to the address Daria had given us. A layer of anticipation and excitement hummed under my skin at the thought of seeing her again. I'd had a hard enough time with one crush, and now I was fully immersed in two of them.

No, that wasn't fair. *Crush* made me think of simple lust. What I felt for both of them was so much more than lust.

We reached the house and parked on the street with a handful of other cars, most of which I recognized from the pool. The man who answered the door looked a lot like Daria. We both knew Dustin, so we exchanged greetings, and he pointed us toward the back of the house.

We were halfway across the main floor when Alana intercepted us. "I'm glad you made it. We need to talk." Her tone was formal and polite. Not a surprise, since she addressed the adults around her like this most of the time.

Was it good or bad that we were currently *adults* and not *friends*? "About what?" I asked.

She looked at Dustin with a scowl. "Go outside."

"Excuse me?" He stared back.

Alana's stern demeanor faltered. "Please? It's private."

Dustin sighed. "All right." He gave us one more glance, then stepped through the sliding glass doors that cut us off from the shouting and laughter on the other side.

"How are you both feeling?" Polite and formal Alana was back. "How's your head?"

"I have the occasional headache, but I'm fine." I'd love to know what she was up to.

"And Tanner, how's your arm?"

He flexed his fingers, but didn't move the shoulder itself. "It'll heal. They don't think I need surgery as long as I'm gentle with it."

"How are you?" I asked Alana. She was obviously in control of this conversation.

She frowned. "I'm concerned."

What?

"How can we help?" Tanner's somber tone matched hers.

"I'm glad you asked. You can take my mom out on a date, so she stops being sad."

Tanner coughed.

I didn't know why he was the least bit surprised to hear Alana be so direct. "We can ask. She has to say *yes*, though."

"She will. I already told her to." Alana sounded confident.

This conversation was both surreal and buoying, and a very large part of me wanted to be enough a part of Daria's life—of her girls' lives—that conversations like this were the norm.

Alana held up a finger. "But keep in mind, if you make my mom sadder, I'll find a different team to swim for, and you'll not only have to replace me, but find someone who thinks they can beat me, and good luck with that."

No wonder she loved having Tanner as a coach.

I half crouched, so I was at her eye-level. "I promise you, the last thing I want—that either of us wants—is to make Daria sad."

"In fact, you and Harmony should join us sometimes when we take her out, to make sure," Tanner added.

Alana seemed to consider this. "You can't bribe us with presents."

"We wouldn't dream of it," I said.

"But that shouldn't stop you from trying." Her words tumbled out quickly.

This wasn't a conversation I expected to have today, but I was glad we had. I extended my hand. "It's a deal. We agree to all of your terms."

"Good." She shook my hand and then Tanner's. "My mom is outside, and she's lonely because she's not swimming. You should do something about that."

I had no arguments.

When we stepped outside, it was as if we were minor celebrities. The friends Alana had invited were almost all students, and everyone wanted to make sure we were all right.

The concern was nice, but I wanted to break away and go talk to the woman standing back from all of it, watching us with amusement playing on her face. She was wearing a one-piece suit and a cover-up that did nothing to hide her gorgeous curves.

"Why isn't anyone swimming?" Dustin called. "I thought this was a pool party."

Daria's smile grew.

Sometimes older siblings were an utter embarrassment, but sometimes they were just the best. The latter was especially true in adulthood.

The group disbursed, and Tanner and I headed toward Daria.

"Hey," she greeted us softly.

All this build-up, and I had no idea what to do next. "Hey."

"I'm glad you made it," she said.

"Like we were going to miss the fun?" Even Tanner sounded a little hesitant. He sighed loudly. "I can't do this. Can we talk about the elephant in the room, and move on?"

I laughed. "And this is one of the reasons I love you." The words slipped out without thought, thanks to the last few days of being immersed in each other.

Daria's eyes grew wide and her jaw dropped. "Did you just— Are you two— Fuck me, it's about time."

"Did everyone know but me?" Tanner asked.

Daria nodded. "Yes."

I squeezed his hand. "But you're pretty even when you're being clueless."

"Thanks." Tanner stuck his tongue out at me.

"*But*"—I looked at Daria—"even though he and I

are together, there's room for one more. Or three more. I don't want you to ignore your kids for us. I'd rather we were a part of your lives, and not the other way around. How do I say that and have it still be inclusive, but also not creepy?"

Daria's smile grew. "I think you just did."

"God, I want to kiss you." So, so badly. "But it seems like we have more talking to do before…"

"We make this public." Tanner picked up the thought without hesitation.

"Yes. To both." Daria gestured to the edge of the pool. "Sit with me instead, and we'll do the talking and probably the kissing too, when things are quieter?"

Could we send everyone home now? Probably not, but it was tempting. "I have a better idea. I'll teach you how to swim."

"No. I don't… No." Daria shook her head.

"He's a really good teacher," Tanner said.

She met my gaze. "All right. Go change." She jerked a thumb toward the pool house. "Then swimming."

She didn't have to tell me twice.

30
daria

ANY ROMANTIC RELATIONSHIP with Colin and Tanner would be more complicated than Alana saying *Mom, you can date them,* and them saying *we want to be a part of your lives.*

More talking had to happen. More making sure the men understood what that meant to me. Making sure I did.

Despite all of that, I finally felt like it was okay to consider the possibility. To look at a future and imagine them being a part of it. To admit I'd fallen for both Tanner and Colin, and I was tired of relegating visits to dropping my kids off for their classes.

Colin hopped into the shallow end of the pool and gestured for me to join him. The water was only up to my chest, so drowning wasn't a concern. I waded toward him.

Growing up, Dustin was a competition swimmer in school. Nothing like Tanner, but similar to what

Alana was currently doing. I'd rebelled against swimming. If my big brother was doing it, I didn't want anything to do with it.

And then it was never a thing anymore. Not a lot of people ask an adult woman *can you swim*? So learning never came up.

Colin took my hands in his, and a shock of want spilled through me. I swallowed the response... mostly.

He searched my face. "Do you trust me?"

"Yes." The answer came more easily than I expected. He probably meant just the lesson, but I trusted him with a lot more, and that was both terrifying and wonderful.

He pulled me closer, turned my side toward him, and settled a hand on the middle of my back. "I won't let you fall in the water. I won't let anything happen to you. Your body will want to tense up, and that's okay, but think through it and make yourself relax."

"Okay." I breathed through my nose. My pulse raced as much from his touch as anything.

Colin pressed his hand closer to my skin. "Lift one leg up. Kick it forward straight."

I did what he said, and an uneasy not-quite weightlessness lapped at my skin.

"Now remember, I've got you," Colin said. "Lift the other leg and lay back at the same time."

I tried to do what he said, but my gut lurched and panic surged inside when I lost all contact with the bottom of the pool. I tried to calm myself, like he'd said, but I wanted to feel the ground under my feet again.

"You're doing good." Colin moved his other arm under my legs, keeping me from returning to an upright position. "I've got you. Straighten your body and breathe."

I forced myself to keep breathing through my nose, despite the water lapping at my ears and back, and the urge to hold my breath until I was standing again.

"Relax." His voice was calm and soothing. "I've got you."

Now I understood why the younger kids liked learning from him. I forced myself to trust his hands, his experience, and I pushed the tension from my body.

"You're doing it." He sounded pleased. "You're floating."

"You're holding me up."

"And I'm going to take the training wheels off, okay?"

I didn't dare shake my head. "Nope. Not okay."

"I'm right here. You've got this." He moved both his hands next to each other, near the small of my back.

I could do this. I was a grown woman for fuck's sake—I could float at the shallow end of a private swimming pool. "I've got this."

Colin moved one hand to mine, and squeezed. Then he moved his other hand away.

Panic flashed inside, and I thought through it. The water didn't rush in to claim my soul, it rocked my body instead, holding me upright as if I were weightless. A laugh slipped from my throat. "I'm floating."

"*Cannon ball.*" The shout from the other end of the pool carried above the laughter and shouts, and my entire world rolled and churned as water splashed me in the face.

My limbs flailed and I inhaled as much water as air.

"I've got you." Colin was there, righting me and making sure my feet found the ground. Keeping his hands on my waist while I hacked up a lung full of water.

How super fucking attractive of me. Not. When I could finally breathe again, I forced out a tight laugh. "I think I'm done with swimming lessons for today."

"We'll do them privately next time."

I looked up to find Colin watching me with adoration, rather than the disgust my undoubtedly red, splotchy face deserved. He really was a keeper.

"I'm not sure I can afford private lessons," I teased, wanting to move on from the embarrassing moment.

He dipped his mouth near my ear, his breath caressing my skin. "I'm sure we can work something out."

There was no way this exchange was escaping all attention, and I was pretty sure I didn't mind. "I'm open to negotiation." But for today, I was happy to wrap up in a towel and join Tanner at the edge of the pool again. Colin sat on his other side, and the three of us watched and chatted for the next couple of hours.

The afternoon crept toward evening, and we pulled everyone out of the pool and wrapped up the party. After everyone else had dressed enough to leave, Colin and Tanner vanished to do the same.

As the last girl was talking to Alana and waiting for her mom to pick her up, I chatted with Adrienne.

Phillip joined us near the patio doors. "You could leave the girls here for the night, if you wanted."

His implication was clear. *Ditch the girls, and go have hot sweaty sex with the cute boys.* Something I swore I'd never do. "I can't."

"It's okay," Adrienne said.

Dustin seemed to appear out of nowhere. "We'll stretch out the party. Watch movies. Color."

"I need new art for my wall. Harmony can help." Adrienne was too sweet.

I shook my head. "I don't think so, but thank you."

"Mom." Alana's soft voice came from behind, startling me.

Where was her sister? I cast a gaze around the patio to find Harmony talking to Colin and Tanner. She was telling them some sort of story that required a lot of hand gestures, and they were listening intently.

A fist clenched around my heart.

"It's not like you're abandoning us," Alana said. "Besides, Phillip has Twinkies in the cupboard."

An infatuation I didn't understand. "You'd ditch me for Twinkies?" I tried to keep my tone light.

"Nope." Alana popped on the *p*. "I won't even let you bribe me with Twinkies. But it really is okay. I promise if this day ever comes up in therapy, I'll only say good things."

I stared at her, and she grinned. "Teasing," she said. She was definitely growing up too fast.

"All right. Go get Harmony and tell her you're having a sleepover at Phillip's house." It wasn't easy to say, but it didn't make me feel as guilty as I dreaded.

As Alana tugged Harmony toward the house, I approached Tanner and Colin. Their warm smiles made my insides flutter. "We still need to have a conversation," I said. "Meet me back at my place?"

They both agreed.

The drive home was a torturous mental assault of me figuring out what I needed to say, and discarding every idea that popped into my head. At the house, it was strange having them here again, but even stranger that they'd knocked rather than let themselves in. But it felt right to see them in my entryway.

As the door closed us off from the outside world, Tanner gripped the back of my neck with his good hand, and crushed his mouth to mine. Heat seared through me, and I pressed back, needing to lose myself in his touch. I'd missed this—missed him—so much more than I'd been willing to admit.

Colin rested a hand on my cheek and stole me away. Stealing a kiss. Stealing my breath.

I could lose myself in this—in them—over and over. Which was why I needed to put a pause on things. Just for a moment.

I stepped out of their reach. "Talking first."

Who knew seeing grown men pout could be so adorable?

We moved to the living room. I waited for them to sit, and took a spot so I could face both of them, close enough for the setting to feel intimate, without being close enough to give into temptation and touch them.

Tanner opened his mouth.

"Me first." I had to get this out now. "That week together, here… *wow*." I was hot just thinking about it. "But if we keep seeing each other, that won't be the norm."

Colin started to say something, and I held up a finger. He snapped his jaw shut.

"What we had before that—the friendship—I don't let a lot of people into my life like that. The girls' lives." I still had no idea how to phrase this, so I was going to let the words pour out and hope they conveyed the right message. "I wouldn't have offered to let you stay here if I didn't like you. If I didn't trust you. This is the home I built for my daughters and I always want them to feel secure here."

Was that it? I could say more, but it would be

repetition. If Colin and Tanner understood what I'd said, we could talk about the rest. I looked between the two of them. "I don't want to ignore what I feel for each of you, but I'm not labeled for individual sale. Alana and Harmony are my heart, and there's room in there for other kinds of love, but not without them. It's easy for someone to say they get that, but I need to know you mean it."

Tanner nodded. "I do. We do."

"But it makes sense that you'd want more than just our words," Colin said. "That you want to see it for yourself."

I could've guessed this is about how they'd respond, but I heard their sincerity, and that meant a lot. "I do want to see this whole thing in action, all of us spending time together." And now the terrifying part. "I love you both. Individually and together. If you shove my girls aside, it won't matter how I feel about you, you'll be gone. But I also wouldn't be talking to you if I couldn't believe the things you say."

Tanner gave a short laugh. "There's so much of you in them. They're very much their mother's daughters."

"Oh?" I liked the observation, but I needed to know where it came from.

"Alana told us if we made you sad, she wouldn't swim for us anymore," Tanner said.

"I think we have her seal of approval," Colin added.

It sounded like it, and that warmed and reassured me. "She thinks the world of you, which makes this both an easier and a harder decision."

Tanner scooted closer and lifted my chin to hold my gaze. "I promise you, this is what I want. I want to be a part of your entire life, including your kids'."

"And I promise I'm happy to prove it." Colin moved to my other side and rested a hand on my leg. "I adore your children. I love you, and I couldn't stop myself from loving you, even if I tried. Trust me, I tried."

"I love you too," Tanner said. "You've got this amazing mind, and you're an incredible woman. Fucking stunning. Clothed. Unclothed." Mischief danced in his eyes.

"*Dude.*" Colin's retort was teasing. "That was almost poetic until the end."

Tanner scoffed. "Fucking someone I love is its own poetry. You're an artist—you understand that."

Warm fuzzies fluttered inside me. This felt good, talking to them and joking with them. It felt right. And now that we had the important conversation out of the way, we could get on to the fun stuff. "We have the house to ourselves for the night. It'd be a shame to waste this opportunity."

Tanner drew his thumb over my cheek "Did I mention the sexy fucking mind? I do like the way you think." He brushed his lips over mine so lightly it was more of a suggestion than a kiss.

I felt it all the way to my toes anyway.

"Did you have something specific in mind?" Colin brushed my hair over one shoulder, and dragged his mouth along the back of my neck. "Or do you want to play it by ear?"

I was very much a *go into things with a plan* person, and it terrified me to play any of this by ear—even a night of sex. But the excitement and anticipation were delicious, and I was eager to see what came next. "Tanner's got a bum arm, so we should probably go easy on him."

"Hmm." Colin's murmur rumbled over my skin. "Fair point."

"I can do more with one good arm than most people can do with both." Tanner scoffed.

I leaned away from him and into Colin. "Like watch?"

"Definitely not. Not today." Tanner knelt to lean into us both. "This is definitely going to be a hand-on kind of evening."

I did have one requirement though. "Bedroom. Door locked." A teensy bit of me both worried and hoped they'd argue—no one else was here, no one was expected to be.

"Agreed." Tanner stood and grasped one of my hands.

Colin was on his feet as well, the two of them tugging me to mine.

When we made it upstairs and closed ourselves off from the rest of the world, I was instantly pulled into a flurry of kisses and touches. Tanner crushing his mouth to mine to devour my groans. Colin stealing me away to nip at my lips, then kiss a trail along my jaw and neck. The two of them pulling into each other in a long kiss that was so easy and natural, and so fucking sexy.

Then their mouths were on me again. I was swept up by the intensity wrapping around all of us, and I wanted more. I'd missed having them here. Feeling them. And I needed more of it. I undid the buttons on Tanner's shirt, hungry for more.

The three of us stripped each other out of everything, pausing every few seconds to kiss or lick or nibble on each other. And when we were finally naked, the heat of our bodies molded together was delicious. I couldn't believe I was a part of this, or that I'd almost had to surrender it.

Tanner moved behind me. He dragged his mouth up my shoulder, along my neck, and paused to nip my earlobes.

I moaned at the delicious sensation and leaned my weight into him for more, letting his erection dig into my ass cheek and tease me.

Colin stayed in front of me, but lowered his head to draw one of my nipples into his mouth. The longer he suckled, the more my hips swayed with need. I clenched my thighs together, but the pulse wouldn't be sated this way.

When Colin glided his hand down my stomach, my anticipation spiked. He dipped between my legs and I gasped at his touch. At the build-up to what came next. He slid lower along my slick skin, and dipped two fingers inside me. I was used to penetration as a main course, not an appetizer, and I liked this variation on an old classic.

The longer Colin pumped inside me, with Tanner trailing his hand over so much of my body, the further I sank into the pleasure. When Colin pulled out, disappointment glimmered inside, but it vanished in a flash when he glided up to trace circles around my clit.

I bucked against the fresh touch against my hyper sensitive sex, and wanted more. The longer he teased and stroked, the more my desire built, until it crashed down around me, spilling through me with climax.

Colin eased his touch away from the swollen nub, and kissed me again. Hard. Hungrily. Devouring my gasps before letting Tanner tug me away for more of the same.

With the initial need dialed to a high simmer, I could imagine next steps. I turned to Tanner. "With that arm, I think you're going to have to be passive in most of this."

"She's right, you know," Colin said.

Tanner raised an eyebrow. "I can do a lot with one arm."

"I promise you'll like this." I pressed a hand to his chest and nudged him toward the bed. "Lie down."

He stared back in disbelief, but complied.

I didn't try to hide the way I raked my gaze over

his nude, prone form. Stunning. Statuesque. Tauntingly erect. "Don't move"

His jaw dropped as I turned away. I felt two pairs of eyes on me as I made my way into the bathroom to grab two condoms and lube from the locked cabinet.

When I returned, my skin was on fire at the heat of their gazes, watching me walk naked across the bedroom. My pulse hammered in my ears and I shrugged off any insecurities about what I did or didn't need to hide.

I handed one rubber to Colin and rolled the other onto Tanner. I slid up Tanner's body, and he moved his good hand to my thigh to squeeze. Every touch sent jolts of want racing over me.

I reached his cock, and glided my still-wet pussy back and forth along the shaft, teasing until he was groaning and digging his fingers into my leg. I rose enough to position him at my opening. His strangled groan as I lowered myself, driving him inside me, was intoxicating.

This was amazing. So very close to perfect. Not just because Tanner was inside me and Colin pressed into my back, sandwiching me between two hot, younger men. The fantasy aspect was off the charts. But even better—I knew these men. Their hearts. Their minds. What they were capable of.

And I knew I wanted them both. In my bedroom, in my life, and in my future.

31
colin

THERE WAS no universe where it wasn't *hot* to watch Daria with Tanner. The way she rode him... I swore I could feel it.

I needed to be part of this connection, though. I knelt behind Daria, my legs digging into Tanner's, and molded myself to her back when I drew her upright. I needed to memorize every inch of flesh on flesh from the three of us intertwined with each other.

The soft curve of her ass cushioned my erection as I glided my hands up her stomach to cup her breasts. She rocked in a gentle rhythm against Tanner. I licked along her shoulder to suck on her neck. "Do you mind if I leave marks?"

Daria's laugh caught me off-guard. "I've never been asked that before."

"I figured given everything..." I didn't want to do anything that would cause friction—hers or mine— with her kids.

"I'm not complaining, and no I don't mind."

I loved the sound of her *yes* as much as the soft gasps she made when I sucked along the soft skin where her neck met her shoulder.

She leaned more of her weight against me and pressed her cheek to mine. "I want you both in me," she said.

"I like the sound of that." I reached past her to grab the lube.

She squealed in surprise when I pressed a cool slick touch to her skin, but relaxed quickly as I teased her opening with my finger. She leaned forward into Tanner, and he spread one cheek. I slipped a digit inside her, helping her loosen up and relax for something bigger.

"The teasing is killing me." Tanner's chuckle was tight.

I completely understood. "Daria?"

She nodded. "Definitely ready. Mostly. Go slowly."

"Of course." I gripped my shaft and nudged the head of my cock against her rear hole.

She relaxed to let me in, and I slid forward one agonizingly slow inch at a time, until she was wrapped around me, tight and hot, Tanner pressing against me.

The rhythmic rocking resumed, slow and steady. I gripped her hip with one hand, and slipped the other between Daria and Tanner to her clit.

Her entire body jumped, and she clenched around

me, when I found my target. Her gasps grew louder, becoming moans, the longer I stroked, and pumped in time with Tanner.

There was a pause where held her breath, and the entire room seemed to freeze for a heartbeat in time. And then the cry that tore from her throat, breathy and reckless, blanketed all of us. The incredible sound snapped a restraint I didn't realize had been holding me back.

I let go, pounding hard and fast, matching Tanner thrust for thrust, as Daria's body shuddered in pleasure. I was lost in the experience, falling into the sparkles that flashed behind my eyelids. Losing myself in her heat. In Tanner's grunts. In the bubble of reality encasing us.

I lost track of where their groans of pleasure ended and mine began, and flew into the ecstasy building inside me. Orgasm flooded my limbs, tightened in my balls, spilled from me, and left my mind blissfully blank.

Tanner's jerking, the sound of his pending climax, was already deliciously familiar, and I knew he was coming too.

The pounding didn't slow until my body demanded it, and even then I was reluctant to stop. There was time. For more of this. For more wrapping myself up in these feelings and these two people. But I was still greedy and wanted more now.

I could wait a little while to recharge. Just a little.

We lay there, sandwiched on top of each other,

until Tanner pointed out his leg was cramping. The three of us disentangled long enough to clean up, then crawled into bed next to each other.

Lying here next to both of them was perfect. "I missed this. I know we won't be doing it all the time. Not yet, but…"

"So you haven't changed your minds." There was a hitch in Daria's voice.

Tanner raised his eyebrows and looked between her and me. "Excuse you, what?"

Daria shrugged. "Now that we've had the dirty, yummy sex and gotten that out of our systems for the night, you're still interested in everything that comes with the package that is Daria?"

"Every single inch of you." He kissed her on the nose.

"You know I mean more than me." She blushed, despite the guarded question.

I didn't know how to make this clearer, beyond reassurance and just proving we meant what we said, but I was happy to assure her again and again. "We do know that, yes. We meant everything we said downstairs. I missed you, I love you, and I want you both—all—in my life."

"Same." Daria's smile was back, lighting up a gorgeous face. "To everything you just said, I feel the same."

"Of course you do," Tanner teased.

She laughed. "Ass."

He kissed her, then leaned past her to brush his lips over mine. "I couldn't be luckier."

Warmth filled me. This was the family I never thought I'd have. Yes, I had Brooke and her kids, and they were great, but this was different. Its own kind of love and closeness. This was what so many people had told me in my life that I didn't deserve, because of my preferences.

But I had it. And even though I wasn't a look-to-the-future kind of guy, I saw all the potential stretching out before us. This was going to be incredible.

32

tanner

I'D BEEN DATING Colin and Daria for almost two weeks, and the experience, the bond, was incredible. I wasn't always a fan of heading home without her at the end of the night, but the fact that I got to go with him helped. And it was both surreal and a blast to head out as a pseudo-family.

Tonight was an excuse to go to Buck E. Cheese without looking like a weird creeper. This place wasn't quite the wonderland I remembered from childhood, but it was still a blast.

Alana had proclaimed she was going to beat me at skeeball, but that I wasn't supposed to hold back.

"My right arm is taped to my side. I don't have a choice but to hold back," I said.

She shrugged. "Sounds like your problem. You never know when battle might happen. You have to be prepared."

"I'm pretty sure that's not how that saying goes."

With some kids, I'd hold back regardless. With my ultra-competitive, star swimmer, there was no way. In her shoes, I'd be offended if I gave anything but my best. I grabbed the first ball with my left hand, and lobbed it easily into a 100 spot.

Alana scoffed. "Amateur." She matched me almost shot for shot. Almost.

"Someone's been training." I was genuinely impressed. I didn't realize kids still played games like this—not that I'd phrase it that way to her.

She scowled and dropped tokens in the two machines, pulling up another round of balls. "Again."

"Alana, don't push him too hard," Daria called from the table a few feet away.

Did that make my manliness bristle just a little, that a thirteen-year-old was supposed to go easy on me? Just a little. "I'm fine." I tossed the first ball.

"See, Mom, he's *fine.*" Alana mimicked the motion.

Behind us, I heard Harmony leading Colin back from the ball pit, while she told him about the next chapter in her unicorn—previously a pony but now ascended—story.

I couldn't help a smile at how comfortable this all was. Like it was meant to be this way. I took my next shot.

Once again, Alana and I were evenly matched. We each had one ball left, and were tied, when my phone rang. A glance at the screen said it was the banker Daria had referred us to. The one we'd been waiting on an answer from for an agonizingly long amount of time. "I need to take this. You win."

"I don't win until I beat you fair and square. Teach me how to throw left-handed?"

"Practice. You know how it works." I called as I walked toward the table. "This is Tanner," I said into the phone.

Daria and Colin both gave me curious looks when I sat at the table. Harmony looked between them, and was silent as well.

"Tanner, hi. It's Stephen Rodgers. I'm sorry to call so late."

"It's fine." My stomach was tying in knots. Even if he said *no* it would be an answer, but I wasn't as prepared for a *no* as I wanted to pretend. "What can I do for you?"

"After some close review of your proposal, your assets, and your expertise, we'd like to work with you on this loan."

My mind had already jumped ahead to *we've decided to go in another direction*, and I had to backtrack to process what he'd really said. "Wait, what? Really?" Not so professional. "I mean, of course. That's fantastic news. Thank you."

Colin's brows shot up, and Daria's smile grew.

"I'll email you the initial paperwork and terms. Once you've reviewed, we can start scheduling appointments and moving forward," Stephen said.

"Yeah. Of course. Thank you." I was repeating myself. I managed to focus enough to wrap up the important details, and end the call professionally. The instant I disconnected I let out a loud *whoop*. "We got the loan. We're getting our school."

"I knew you would." Daria grinned.

"We had someone amazing help us finalize our plans." I owed her so much thanks for this.

She shook her head. "The best proposal doesn't hide a shitty idea. You have a great plan, I just put a bow on it."

Colin hadn't said anything.

I didn't like that. "Colin?" Had this changed his mind?

He finally broke into the biggest smile. "It's about time. This is going to be freaking epic."

"Freaking epic. Freaking epic," Harmony sang a tuneless melody.

And Colin was right—like usual. Getting the business loan was amazing, but this dynamic here, this family, *this* was better than epic. This was a better future than I ever would've dared imagine.

epilogue

Daria

Eight Months Later

The Grand Reopening sign was a generic banner—something Tanner picked up at a store—but it made me smile to see it decorating the front of the rec center.

The building had been closed for several months, but since a lot of that was over the fall and winter months, Colin and Tanner had already expected the loss in clients. I was amazed they'd pulled together the full remodel in such a short amount of time. And now that they'd fixed up the entire building, not just the pool, they'd be open year-round going forward.

The place had been unofficially open for a month or so, with the new instructors and trainers all getting used to the schedules. Tanner was doing as much swimming as he was allowed, and pretending not to sulk when other trainers had to take on more of the load. But he was healing nicely from the surgery and he'd be back to almost full strength soon enough.

Colin wasn't teaching much swimming, though he did have one younger class. He was teaching art classes, which Harmony loved since she'd gotten bored with swimming. He had a few after school programs for the younger kids, and they all adored him.

Tonight was a school expo of sorts, including a swimming match to let the older students show off, and draw in new families. Alana had been talking non-stop for weeks about competing. Tanner never treated her differently than the other swimmers in class, not giving her leniency or making things harder on her.

She ate up the fairness of it all. If she was going to win, it would be because she earned it. And she was going to win—she said so on a regular basis.

Both girls had come early with Colin and Tanner, to finish set-up. I'd tried to talk them out of it, but all of them insisted it would be fine.

Inside, I found Carly with Brooke, who we'd become good friends with over the past few months. They were walking from the gym toward the pool, both of them with small plates heaped with brownies and cookies.

"I don't think you're supposed to bring those into the pool area," I said, falling into step with them.

Carly shoved a brownie at me, and picked a cookie from her stack. "I guess we'd better eat them before we get there, then." She shoved the entire thing in her mouth.

Brooke snorted and shook her head. "Match starts in just a few minutes."

"Dmnit," Carly mumbled through cookie crumbs. She wrapped the rest of her plate in a napkin, and set it gently on the top of her purse.

I couldn't help but laugh. "If you had kids, that wouldn't be safe in there for even ten seconds." I ate the brownie quickly, though not as fast as she'd managed with her sweet.

Carly swallowed. "Reason number seven-thousand-ninety-two why I don't." She hugged her purse to her chest. "No one better step on this."

We stepped into the pool area, where people were already gathering on the bleachers. I saw Alana with Tanner and her team, at the far end of the pool, and waved. When we were settled, I sent Colin a text. *We're here.*

Be there soon, his reply came through seconds later.

Carly, Brooke, and I settled into a spot big enough for us plus two more, and Carly nudged me. She jerked her head toward the door.

Joe was here. I expected to feel a surge of emotion. Instead a little pity and disdain flitted in, but not much more.

"Is it true?" Carly asked.

I studied my ex-husband from across the room. His face was drawn, and the bags under his eyes were visible from here. He was dressed in jeans, which I think I'd seen maybe twice since we got married. The threat I'd made months ago, to ruin his career... He hadn't needed my help. "Is what true?" I asked innocently.

Carly raised her eyebrows. "You know what."

"I don't gossip." Which was why I knew this and she didn't. It had been killing me to keep this to myself, but I almost felt bad that there was a hint of smugness when I thought about it. Almost.

"You're fucking kidding me right now," Carly said.

I sighed. "It's true. He was caught screwing the boss's daughter." Adult daughter. Barely. She was twenty-two, and I hoped for her sake that she'd learned and moved on to someone better. "It's my understanding that he can't get anyone to take his calls."

Brooke sucked in a breath. "Ouch."

"I mean... No one made him put his dick in her, so—"

"*Daddy,*" Harmony's shout cut me off, and I immediately homed in on my girl, in the hallway and speed-walking toward the doorway.

Joe's face lit up and he turned toward the sound.

Harmony cut in a completely different direction, toward Colin, and handed him a large sheet of paper I assumed was her latest artwork. Colin smiled and crouched to bring himself to her eye-level. She was too far away for me to hear anything softer than a yell, but the way she waved her arms and her animated expressions led me to believe she was telling him the story behind the picture.

"He really is cute with her," Carly said.

I couldn't agree more. Colin and Tanner were both good with the girls. I loved that they helped around the house, but more I loved that they were there, and part of the family. I could tell they meant it. That they loved me. Loved the kids. Loved each other. I never would've imagined something like this was possible even with one guy, especially after Joe, but I wouldn't trade what I had with these men.

Harmony grabbed Colin's hand and tugged him toward us. She paused long enough to wave at Joe, then climbed up the bleachers to sit between Colin and me. "Mommy, it's us in Italy." She handed me her drawing.

We hadn't been yet, but as soon as Harmony overheard me talking to Carly about maybe making the trip, she'd started with the plans. I took the picture from her, and sure enough, all five of us were standing in a row, in front of... I pointed to the large, tower-like thing in the background. "Tell me about this," I said.

"That's the Eiffel tower." Harmony said. "And the Ferris wheel. And the opera house." She pointed at the different images.

I knew if I looked at Carly, she'd either be wincing or trying to swallow a laugh. A glance past Colin, at Brooke, showed a soft smile playing on her face.

"Let's have a geography story when we get home," Colin suggested.

Harmony clapped. *Lessons* were no fun, but *stories* about where famous architecture actually lived was very much her thing.

A whistle echoed through the room, and the loud chatter died to a low roar. A voice came over the loud-speaker—one of Tanner's new swim coaches—announcing the start of the exhibition match. The races were fast-paced and intense. Single elimination, narrowing down the swimmers until there were two left.

Alana made it all the way to the finals, and came in a heartbeat behind the winner. Her scowl was obvious from here, and I knew this was going to hurt. As far as she was concerned, second place was first loser.

But she was gracious with her smile and shaking the other girl's hand, before they ran off to the locker rooms to change.

After the awards ceremony, and everything broke up, we drifted back to the gym where the refresh-ments were. Carly already had her cookies back out and was pleased they weren't crushed. She even offered one to Harmony, who looked at me question-ingly before accepting.

Tanner and Alana joined us a few minutes later. Carly and Brooke congratulated her.

Her smile was tighter up close. "Thank you,"

Alana was polite. "But I'll actually deserve it next time."

"You'll kick butt, next time." Tanner said.

Alana scoffed. "Yeah, I will." She glanced over her shoulder, then looked at me. "Can I go say hi to Joe?"

I didn't bother to correct her. "Do you want company?"

"I'll be fine."

"Can I go with?" Harmony asked.

Alana nodded, and took her hand. I may be smug that Joe had screwed himself out of work, but I didn't ever want the girls hurting because of it. Alana and Harmony walked toward him.

He smiled when he saw them. The hug from Harmony was genuine and sweet, but the one with Alana was wooden and awkward. Whatever the three had to talk about didn't take long. As Alana and Harmony turned away from him, he walked out of the room.

When the girls reached us again, Alana asked, "Can I have a cookie? And go talk to my friends?"

"We should probably do the same. The mingling thing," Tanner said.

"Then shoo. All of you." I made waving motions, then took Harmony's hand when the other three scattered.

"You all really are good together." Was that wistfulness in Carly's voice?

Brooke sighed softly. "You really are. You're lucky, you know."

I did know. Everything about my relationship with Tanner and Colin, and theirs with Harmony and Alana, was right. This was the way life should be. A life I wouldn't give back for anything.

Thank you for falling in love along with Daria, Colin, and Tanner.

For more sexy, geeky threesomes, and to meet Daria's brother, Dustin, check out RANDOM ENCOUNTER. Adrienne is starting her dream job as a video game artist. But the game requires her to recreate some intimate and kinky bedroom scenes, and she's lacking experience. Fortunately, her sexy co-workers have her back... her front... and everything in between with hands-on lessons.